THE HEMINGWAY CAPER

THE
HEMINGWAY
CAPER

ERIC WRIGHT

A Castle Street Mystery

THE DUNDURN GROUP
TORONTO · OXFORD

Editor: Barry Jowett
Copy-editor: Rachel Sheer
Design: Jennifer Scott
Printer: Webcom

National Library of Canada Cataloguing in Publication Data

Wright, Eric
 The Hemingway caper / Eric Wright.

ISBN 1-55002-451-5

I. Title.

PS8595.R58H44 2003   C813'.54   C2003-901650-1   PR9199.3.W66H44 2003

1   2   3   4   5   07   06   05   04   03

Canada

THE CANADA COUNCIL | LE CONSEIL DES ARTS
FOR THE ARTS | DU CANADA
SINCE 1957 | DEPUIS 1957

ONTARIO ARTS COUNCIL
CONSEIL DES ARTS DE L'ONTARIO

We acknowledge the support of the **Canada Council for the Arts** and the **Ontario Arts Council** for our publishing program. We also acknowledge the financial support of the **Government of Canada** through the **Book Publishing Industry Development Program** and **The Association for the Export of Canadian Books**, and the Government of Ontario through the **Ontario Book Publishers Tax Credit** program, and the **Ontario Media Development Corporation's Ontario Book Initiative.**

Care has been taken to trace the ownership of copyright material used in this book. The author and the publisher welcome any information enabling them to rectify any references or credit in subsequent editions.

J. Kirk Howard, President

Printed and bound in Canada.⊛
Printed on recycled paper.
www.dundurn.com

Dundurn Press
8 Market Street
Suite 200
Toronto, Ontario, Canada
M5E 1M6

Dundurn Press
73 Lime Walk
Headington, Oxford,
England
OX3 7AD

Dundurn Press
2250 Military Road
Tonawanda NY
U.S.A. 14150

For Joe Kertes,
who encourages this kind of thing

chapter one

"*The rain began again as I turned onto Harbord
Street and brought the car to a stop in front of
Poppy's bar.*"

No.

"*The rain began again as I turned onto Harbord Street
and stopped in front of Poppy's bar.*"

Better.

"*The rain began and I turned onto Harbord Street
and jammed my foot down hard on the brake and
switched off the ignition and the headlights. It was
warm in the car and soon I could not see through the
steamed-up windows, not even the lighted sign for
Poppy's bar. The rain came down harder and drummed
on the roof of the car and the drops fell like individual
stones in the pools along the gutter.*"

Okay, except for those stones. Take out "individual".

"*I stepped on the brake pedal in front of Poppy's bar ...*"
(The brake pedal in front of Poppy's bar? Shit.)

"*In front of Poppy's bar I stepped on the brake pedal.
I switched off the wipers but it did not make any difference
except to the sound inside the car.*"

Now I've lost it again.

You see what I'm trying to do? Maybe not. It's a riff, I think.
(The word isn't in my processor's memory, but I think that's
what it is.) On Hemingway. Would you have known that if
I hadn't told you? So far I think I've got enough "and"s in
there but the rhythm isn't quite right, so you might not have
guessed what I was up to. I would have to go into parody to
be sure you would recognize it, and parody is another thing.

My name is Joe Barley. I'm employed by a detective agency on
a part-time basis for some of their simpler assignments, like
watching people suspected of insurance fraud who claim to be
incapacitated after an accident. My job is to get pictures of
these villains hang-gliding, or hot-dogging on the ski slopes.

  At present I'm on a very old-fashioned assignment. A
suspicious wife has hired the agency to collect evidence of
her husband's adultery. What she'll do with it I don't
know, because she doesn't need it these days to get a
divorce. She is probably just satisfying herself that her suspicions are justified.

  I've been watching this guy every Tuesday and Thursday
night for three weeks, and so far it certainly seems like a simple case of a bit on the side. His name is Jason Tyler, a book
dealer, specializing in rare and second-hand books. He has a
shop on College Street that occupies two floors of an old
house. His wife thinks he is having an affair because he
recently joined a health club to work out twice a week. She
suspects that on Tuesdays and Thursdays he actually comes
home damp from another kind of work-out, so she has hired
the agency to find out.

  It's a clever front he's constructed. He really does go to
a health club to pedal away for half an hour and have a
shower. Then he spends an hour in a rented room on the
second floor of a small commercial property on Harbord.

Tonight was typical. I was sitting in my car as he arrived in his yellow Volvo, parked in the alley, and entered the side door of this building, the tenants' entrance, making his presence on the second floor known by switching on the light and lowering the blinds. A little later, the shadows of him and a lady appeared behind the blind, embracing in silhouette. After a bit of this, the light went out, the blind was raised, and twenty minutes or so later, the light came back on, the blind was lowered, and the silhouettes again embraced. (I've figured out that they must make love by streetlight). Then, the window blind was raised and I caught a glimpse of them in a quick, unscreened embrace before the light went out again and the two of them re-appeared at the side door for a hasty peck as they went their separate ways.

I followed him as he drove back to his store on College, and made a note of the time so I could finish my report at home—in the "officialese" of a detective agency, of course. Making up a report in Hemingway-speak, so to speak, is just something I do for myself, to keep from getting bored.

Not just Hemingway. I started with Hemingway, because that's where everyone starts. I'm just learning. I work with a voice until I get it, or give up, then move on to a different voice. So far on this job I've tried Jane Austen, Salinger (easy, and so the choice of every pastiche creator), and typical-Russian-short-story ("At midnight, on a certain street in the provincial town of _____, a young man who was due to fight a duel at dawn the next day stood picking his nose and writing in a notebook by the light of the street lamp. He had not eaten for three days, sustained only by the occasional glass of kvass."). It's the sound of the prose, the tone, the rhythm, I'm trying to capture, the music; it doesn't matter if the street lamp shines in a literary cul-de-sac. The plot can wait.

Most of these pastiches don't work, I know that, but trying for them keeps me awake. I really think I caught a whiff of old Ernest for a moment there.

chapter two

Home for me is an apartment in the Annex, which I share with my partner, Carole, a translator who works mainly for the politicians in The Buildings.

Her work is easy, because the things English-speaking politicians want to say to their French-speaking constituents are very simple and have already been said. A cabinet minister who trusts Carole, and remembers that he has been applauded for one of her speeches before, will ask her for "the two founding nations" speech, adapted for a Noelville audience; a speech she can paste together from her files. Actually, most of the speeches she writes are about language in some way or other. One, entitled "Small Business is Big Business," congratulates its French-speaking audience on being able to trade in any language they like, because this government, unlike the government in some other provinces (one, actually) does not demand that they favour one language over another. In Ontario, the speech says, both cultures are respected.

It's pure bullshit, of course. The fact is, if you're French, you have to learn English, but if you speak only English, you can manage just fine, even if you live in Noelville. There has never been a serious effort to foster bilingualism in this province, in the schools or anywhere else. Any premier who wants to put my money where his mouth is could simply require that a competency in French be a requirement for graduation from an Ontario high school. Carole says that if the Conservatives had ordered it done at the height of the separatist agitation, we would now be bilingual, and Ontario residents might be able to read the Montreal newspapers and get a real understanding of what being a French-Canadian is all about. It's not something you'll ever understand in translation, she says. But they didn't, nor did the Liberals who followed them, or the socialist NDP who followed them.

Which is why Carole will always be able to find work. Carole, from long dealing with the people in The Buildings, doesn't have a political twitch left in her nervous system (she no longer votes), and doesn't mind what they ask her to write. She says she writes speeches that will "play", never mind the content. Her favourite model is the Mark Antony "honourable men" speech. Her biggest success with this model was with the one she adapted for the Junior Minister of what was then called Extra-Urban Affairs (something about this title must have clanged in someone's ear because the name changed several times before the civil servants finally settled on Non-Urban Areas, rejecting a suggestion by a wit in the Green Party of "Minister for Country Matters.")

The speech Carole wrote, or rather assembled from stock, was built around the phrase, "I don't know" ("Je ne sais pas"). She had noticed that no politician ever used the phrase in case it came out wrong in French, but the right man, she felt, could create rhetoric out of it. He could alert his audience by intoning it, moving through a series of non-substantive issues, after each one echoing "Je ne sais pas" followed by a significant pause. Then, finally, he would say what he *did* know, bellowing out the positive, "Mais ceci je sais"(never mind the poor accent), or simply showing his fearlessness ("Je n'ai pas peur de vous," etc …).

Simple stuff and not original, but it gave Carole a new interest in her work. The Junior Minister used the speech for about three months, and only when he began to hear one or two of his colleagues pick it up, did he ask Carole to design a new one.

She was sitting up in bed, reading, when I got home, and I, slightly ignited by the touch of voyeurism I had experienced through the book dealer's window, forwent my nightly last look at the television news, and joined her.

She held up the book "Four pages," she said.

"Don't you have a bookmark?"

"Four pages," she repeated.

I sighed, but I wasn't feeling thwarted enough to tear the book from her and fling it across the room, while ripping open the lacy bodice of her nightgown with the other hand. (Actually her preferred sleeping attire is a calico shift like a flour sack, which makes her look like an inmate of a madhouse in one of those French films set in the Middle Ages; and as for tearing it off her, it would take a qualified sail-maker to find the place to make a start.) But I didn't fancy hanging about for four pages either, feeling myself, as I said, only minimally ignited. Instead, I turned to my copy of Boswell's *Johnson*, my bedside reading for as long as I can remember, and soon we were breathing in unison, back to back, I asleep, she reading.

This is the place to note that Carole and I long ago agreed—perhaps it was why we set up house together—that neither of us would yearn silently, a seething mass of frustration, but speak up whenever and however desire manifested itself. She once mistakenly believed me to be yearning for the exotic and did her best to respond (we suit each other in most ways, after all, and we like living together very much) by trying to surprise me with the soles of her feet before she had smoothed them with an emery board, and another time, for the same reason (to give me a surprise), by sharpening her fingernails.

I found the effect in both cases more distracting than stimulating, so she quit experimenting and we concentrated on just holding back the dawn until we were both ready to greet it. So you won't find in what follows any sexual gymnastics, and no fine writing on the subject, either; no detailed descriptions of love's mansion, or any magnificent members bursting into the chamber of delight. None of that. We enjoy a private life crowned with warm endeavours, occasionally begun because of something Carole has read, but never continued to the point of plagiarism.

chapter three

The next morning, Carole kicked me out early.

Ours is a one-bedroom apartment on Howland, in a neighbourhood inhabited mainly by therapists of various kinds, and by freelance creative types—writers, actors, and stand-up comedians. The rent is low, but you have to park on the street and at night, coming back from a movie, it can take some time to find a space, and you get dinted more than you would in, say, Forest Hill. This is the main reason why people with car fetishes, the owners of Mercedes, for instance, and the four-wheel drive crowd, always move away once they've sold a couple of scripts.

As for me, the Toyota van I drive is dinted enough for me not to even notice if I get another scratch. Plus, I appreciate the district's other amenities. To the south, on Bloor Street, we have probably the best strip of good, cheap restaurants in the core of the city, including Mel's, a corned beef restaurant that is open all night and will sell you a half-sandwich if you're not very hungry. And opposite Mel's is Book City, one of the few independent bookstores left now that the chains have gobbled each other up. So we like it here.

As well as the single bedroom we have a bathroom so cramped because of the shower we've installed that you have to close the door to pee even when no one is home, and if you don't lock it you are liable to be knocked off your aim if someone walks in suddenly. (Carole suggests I cultivate the practice of sitting down on all occasions, but that way I would fear being kneecapped until I got in the habit of locking the door.)

So we have one real bedroom, and another tiny room I call my office—an unwelcoming space with no natural light or feeling for which way is north. At night I don't mind it so much, but I can't work there during the day. Then there's the living room, which has a window that looks out on to a brick wall three feet away, so it is usually dusk by noon. And finally, incongruously, there is the kitchen, a big room with a big table and two big windows, one on each side. This is my ideal workroom unless Carole is home and needs it, as she did that morning.

So I left a couple of hours early and drove over to Harbord, to the love nest. I was curious to see it in daylight, and, if possible, to get a look inside.

The building housed three stores on the ground floor: a dollar store selling junk, a video rental place, and a flower shop. The woman selling flowers told me the landlord lived upstairs; I walked round the building to a side door and pressed the bell. After a while, the door opened and a small, friendly-looking man with an unshaven, Geppetto-like face, a man in his late seventies or very early eighties, smiled a greeting, saying nothing.

"My name is Joe Barley," I said "And I'm looking for a room to use as an office."

He inclined his head backwards, still smiling. He was one of those people so at home in the world that he had no suspicions of it, or of me. "What do you do?" he asked.

"I'm a writer," I said. "I can't work at home with all the kids running around so I'm looking for an office."

"What kinds of things you write?"

We might have been chatting over a beer. "Freelance stuff at the moment, but I'm planning a novel."

"A *novel!*" He made a "shooshing" noise like S.K. Sakall, wondering. "Where do you live, then, that you got so much noise?"

Geppetto wasn't right. He looked the part still, but his words were tinged by his upbringing in some East European shtetl.

"On Markham." I grabbed for the name of a street, faintly associated with writers. "South of College," I said, to give it some distance from Honest Ed's, Toronto's biggest bargain house. I remembered that Katie Mountbatten, a sometime colleague of mine at the university, lived there so it must still be affordable.

"Not too far away," Geppetto said, consideringly. "Be a nice walk for you if the weather's good."

"Do you have a room vacant?"

Now he looked me up and down. "Yes," he said. "Yes, I do." He nodded and said again, "Yes. Yes, I have a room. Go to the other end of the building. I'll meet you there." He closed the door in my face gently, slowly, smiling at me as he disappeared.

I walked around the building to where he was already waiting for me with the door open. "I never answer a knock on this door," he said. "There's a fire door connecting this end of the building with my apartment," he said. "But the tenants must not use it."

"Why?"

"It's a *fire* door. I wouldn't have a door at all if it wasn't for the fire department. If someone wants me, including the tenants, they use the door at the other end."

I let it go. We went up the stairs to a narrow corridor linking six rooms: three in the front, on the street side, and three at the back. He opened a door to a back room bare of furniture, with a window overlooking a yard full of junk: two filing cabinets, a rusting set of shelves, a broken water cooler, a bicycle wheel, and so on.

"No furniture," I said, looking round.

"I never get it right. I put in a desk and chair and the tenant turns out to be a masseur, asks me to take them out. The furnishings. I store a few bits in the basement. What did you want the room for? What did you say?"

My mind was on Jason Tyler as he spoke, and I nearly said, "book dealer," but I caught it. "Remember?" I said, "I'm a writer. My wife doesn't understand me. She keeps talking to me, especially between the hours of nine and five, when I'm trying to write. I need a room where she can't get at me."

"A book writer?"

"I'm working up to that."

"*Reader's Digest*, like?"

"That's the idea. So I need a room with a window overlooking the street so I can see life as I write about it." I glanced over my shoulder, along the corridor. I had to hope no one was listening. "Are all your rooms in the front taken?"

"When do you need it?"

"Right away. As soon as I can get it."

"I may have one in a couple of weeks." He paused, scratched his bottom, paused again, gave me a twinkle, looked around in case anyone had sneaked into the corridor in the last few minutes, then trotted decisively to the middle door of the three-in-front, unlocking it. "Quick," he said, more or less whispering. "Take a peek, but stay close to the door. I don't want the tenant walking by outside and seeing you in the room."

There was very little to peek at: a trestle table, a straight-backed office chair, an old armchair; against a wall, a single metal army-style cot with a mattress, a blanket, and a pillow. A towel hung on the back of the door, and a wastebasket stood under the table.

"What does he do?"

"Can't you guess?"

There was no sign of any occupation. The table was bare, the wastebasket empty except for a scrap of paper. There was no phone, no pencils, pens, or paper. "Probably an undercover man for the Secret Service," I guessed. "He's just using the room for surveillance."

Geppetto stepped into the room so he could see out over the street. As he stepped forward I swiftly retrieved the scrap of paper from the wastebasket.

"Who's he watching, I wonder? Maria who runs the fruit stand? The baker? Maybe the dress shop across the street?" Geppetto chuckled to show he was being ironical. "He says he's a writer, like you. Only he never seems to get any ideas. Lately I don't bother to clean this room. Once-a-week cleaning is included in the rent, but there's never anything to clean. A bit of dust. And, yes, I've seen the light on once or twice in the evening, but he's never here in the daytime. What kind of writer is that?"

"I told you, the writer thing is just a front. He's an undercover agent for the C.S.I.S. Clever. What makes you think he'll be leaving?"

"I don't think it's working for him. I know you're joking me with that undercover stuff. I don't mind. I mean, a writer with an empty wastebasket? I do a bit of writing myself, putting together the family history. Sometimes it takes me three or four tries to tell some-one's story, one of my great-uncles who served in the Italian army in the first war, for example. What would the retreat from Caporetto be like for a Jewish baker? Makes for a lot of waste paper. I think that the man believes, like you, that if he has a room of his own, something might happen. That's as close to a writer as he's got. But it hasn't happened. There's a lesson to you, there. Maybe you shouldn't waste your money until you're on the second draft."

"What do you care?"

"I like people to stay awhile. And would this furniture do you? He saw the cot in the basement and asked me if he could use it, for taking a nap, he said. But I don't see how he could ever have got tired."

"As a matter of fact, it would do me fine. So what do you think? How long?"

"I'm guessing he might be gone pretty soon. It looks to me as if he's given up. You want to hear from me when he gives his notice? I've got a week's advance rent. You pay the same."

I fished out an old card I had picked up at a restaurant, crossed out the address and wrote my name and office number at the college. I would have preferred to use a pseudonym but I didn't think Geppetto would be interested in finding out about me. If he did, and told any of my colleagues he was my landlord, and what he believed I was doing in the room, I would confess.

"And your name?" I asked.

"*Glink*a," he said, emphasising the first syllable. "*Glink*a. That's my name."

Confess to my colleagues at Hambleton College, that is, that, like them, I'm writing a novel.

chapter four

Hambleton College is where I hold down my other part-time job, that of sessional lecturer in the English Department. The word "sessional" signifies that my contract lasts only to the end of the session, or term, and to keep me reminded of that they pay me by the hour, unlike the tenured gang who are paid by the year. Of course, I have to teach the leftovers, whatever the tenured faculty don't want, which can be dismaying. Last term I was given a week's notice to prepare "Modes of Satire 1: Theoretical," a course for which forty students had signed up and the asshole who dreamed up the course had disappeared on sabbatical to Dublin to do research for a book tentatively called, "Complaint in Catholic England—A Medieval Safety Valve."

But with a bit of ingenuity, an awareness that the man in Dublin and his course objectives could be ignored, and the security of knowing that I was the only one teaching the course, setting the exam, and marking it, I scraped together an outline. I started with a bit of Donne, wallowed in Swift, and ended up with as much Evelyn Waugh as I thought I could get away with, with a dollop of Vonnegut as dessert. When planning to teach such a course, you keep your eye out for anything that might be useful the next time the merry-go-round throws off "Satire" and you are in the way.

I am digressing, I know, so I'll conclude this rant by admitting that the present situation actually suits me very well. I have been a sessional at Hambleton for long enough to have become the most senior temporary instructor in the department. I have my pick of the bits left out for the dog after the tenured faculty have taken what they want, and I can generally find something appetizing enough in the leavings, filling up if necessary on an extra section of the first year Arts (General) course, one I have always liked teaching.

Because I do like my job—I like teaching English literature; that is, I like talking about prose, poems, and plays, especially to students. I don't have any method, and I don't have any theories. I just tell students about the interesting things I've noticed in the works on the course, and then think of exam questions that will let them do the same.

What I am not is a scholar. I was not able to summon up the interest or, to be honest, the learning, to finish my one attempt at a doctoral thesis, so I am never going to get a full-time job. Our universities, aping the Americans, who themselves set up their universities in the nineteenth century in imitation of the Germans (except for the duelling and calling each other "Doctor/Doctor"), regard a Ph.D as an essential qualification. I understand it's happening in Britain now, too.

On the other hand, unless my tenured colleagues are prepared to do much more teaching than they presently do instead of concentrating on "research" (which, to be fair, they are forced to do by the system), I have a temporary job for life, or until I finish my novel.

Two years ago, I shared an office with a man named Richard Costril, another sessional and an angry man if ever there was one, who, when accused of discriminating against an Abyssinian student, turned the tables on his accusers so adroitly (with my help) that they gave him a tenured appointment with six years' seniority, beginning with a sabbatical, to shut him up. Now Richard's fire has gone out, and he sits among the ashes trying to think of something to turn into a little article to put in his annual report to his chairman. I don't want that to happen to me.

My current office mate is from Scunthorpe, in northern England. When we first shook hands he said, "When I go home they say the coont's back in Scoonthorpe." After he had explained the joke, or rather, re-articulated it in a dialect I could understand, I realized that he was just characterizing himself, not as witty, but as earthy.

He had been hired for a year right off the boat by a fundamentalist church-affiliated college in Manitoba, then let go for comparing the world's belief systems, and for pointing out that historically there had been a lot less blood spilled on God's behalf in Tibet than there had been in Rome or Canterbury. He applied to the graduate school in Toronto, eventually ran out of money, and found work at Hambleton while he continued his thesis. His specialty, his field, is the literature of imaginary travels in the eighteenth century. As far as I understand it, he is trying to trace the common routes the imagination of the day took in the writing of *faux* travel literature, back to where the imagination found its sources. I think that's what he's doing: We don't talk about it much.

When he's in the real world you might mistake him for a character on *Coronation Street*, although when I hinted at that early in our relationship he got very offended. Apparently he's from the other side of England, and for him the characters on *Coronation Street* are all a bit soft. He, and the world he comes from, is hard; he is a hard man from the world of Rugby League football, whatever that is. I've never seen it, even on television. Ernie (we began by calling him Ernest, but he quickly asked if we were taking the piss—his phrase) said that true enough he had been christened Ernest but from the time he was five he had thumped anyone who dared to call him that. His name was "Ernie". Actually, he said, when the subject first arose, he preferred "Ginger". It's an obvious nickname because he's a light pink colour with bright blue eyes, freckled, and covered with thick ginger fuzz, not only on his head but on all the other bits that show where his clothes end.

The name took some getting used to, especially if you wanted to catch his attention from any distance. He asked me early on why everyone seemed to pause before they said his name, like, "You going for coffee, er, Ginger?" While I was trying to think, I told him that Ginger as a colouring was probably not as common in Ontario as it was in Yorkshire, and, actually, as a name, it was more usually attached to girls, exotic cats, and boutiques.

"That's why they say it poncey-like?" he said. "I thought they were taking the piss."

Ginger sees piss-takers everywhere.

I think he's playing a role, being a character, not quite a stage Yorkshireman, though he can do that, too, but, as I say, he's a hard man surprised to find himself in the softest of worlds.

In his job interview, which I was allowed to attend (but not to vote at), there was barely a trace of dialect, and the suit was blue, the shirt white, the tie striped. As soon as he got the job he changed into a knobbly mud-coloured cardigan which he claims his Gran knit him when he said he was coming to Canada, a khaki shirt, moleskin trousers held up by a wide leather strap, and the kind of boots good for striking sparks off cobblestones. He has worn the same outfit ever since, although I assume he must have several similar shirts.

Occasionally, when he wants to create a comic effect, he talks in stage dialect—"is tha coomin' down t'road lud"—although normally his slightly flattened vowels are the only trace of his pre-university background. He's Alan

Bennett in boots, but the man from Scunthorpe is still there. He has a couple of pals from home here in Toronto, and occasionally, if he doesn't want anyone to know what he's talking about, he drops his voice on the phone and slips into real dialect, and then he's unintelligible.

I felt sorry for him when he first moved in with me. He seemed to be someone who could use a lot of help socially, an odd duck in spite of his impersonation of an academic at his interview, certainly someone whom women would find weird. So I took him home for dinner, to Carole's dismay, because she doesn't like cooking. But I wanted to do my bit for the new boy, and I even had the idea we might have a party, that Carole might invite some girl friends to meet him. Carole said she didn't have any girl friends, which I should have known if I had thought about it. After I took Ginger home, she told me I was wasting my time, anyway, though she refused to say why. "You'll see," was all I could get out of her.

chapter five

I did see two weeks later when I surprised Ginger enjoying the assistant to the Dean of Continuous Learning, on his desk. There had been a little get-together in the Continuous Learning division to introduce that session's new faculty, and Ginger, whose workload included tutoring extramural students who needed help in writing essays, had there met the assistant to the dean and carted her off to his lair.

When I told Carole she laughed. "I wondered who he would pick first," she said. Her remark told me once again that I know nothing important about the people I know. And then, two weeks later, I went down to the office one Sunday afternoon to pick up some grade sheets and I found him with a woman who teaches "Movement" in the Theatre department, on the floor this time.

I couldn't leave it there. The next morning I asked him, "If the assistant to the dean finds out about the Movement teacher, isn't life going to be difficult?"

"For her, you mean?"

"For *you*, for Christ's sake."

"Why? I'm not planning to marry either of them. If one of them does find out, she can tell me to fook off, if she wants. Look, let's go down to the canteen at twelve and compare sexual etiquette in Scarborough and Scunthorpe; until then, I've got to get this bloody essay marked."

"One last thing. Don't you have a home? I mean, this isn't anyone's idea of a bower of bliss, is it?" I waved a hand around the shabby office, which isn't even carpeted. His duffel coat had been used to protect the Movement teacher from splinters.

He wrote something on the essay he was reading, put down his pen, and crossed his hands on top of his head. "I live in a residence for postulants for the Catholic Church, a seminary, like, because it's very cheap. Actually I get my board and room free in exchange for light janitorial duties, like cleaning the toilets and shovelling snow. I'm trying to make ends meet on the pittance they are paying me around here. In answer to your question, it's a very liberal house, this residence; there's only one rule—no women allowed past the front door. Now, will you shut up for ten minutes?" He picked up his pen, blew a piece of fluff from the point, and went back to work.

So now, whenever I use the office after hours, I spend a lot of time fumbling with the door key. But I've never found Ginger at home and busy since that day.

I don't think he will be here very long. His other characteristic, related, surely, to his libido, is that he gets into fights. Twice so far, he's appeared on a Monday with a cut lip and a bruised face which, he says, happened in a pickup rugby game he gets involved in on Sundays in High Park, but privately he confessed to me that they were both caused by someone in a bar, "taking the piss".

Ginger doesn't fit the academic mould, even the Hambleton approximation, and yet he's much more of a scholar than I am: he's been seen coming out of the Rare Books room of Robarts Library. He just doesn't look like one.

When I arrived the next morning, Ginger was waiting with a surprise for me. Our furniture—my desk and the old trestle table they had found for Ginger, and our joint filing cabinet—had been rearranged to make room for another table and chair. Ginger pointed to the door. A third name had been added to ours, printed in large, word processed letters and cello-taped to the door. "M. KINOSHITA". We had a new roommate.

This was no surprise. As part-timers we were constantly kept aware of our lack of status. They wouldn't have simply moved another person into the office of a tenured faculty member, but those rules—of courtesy, respect, etc.—don't apply to us.

"Japanese?" I asked Ginger, as I stood there with my back to the doorway.

Ginger nodded. A small smile.

"Met him yet?"

Ginger nodded.

"What's the 'M' stand for?"

Now Ginger was grinning out loud, as it were. "Masaka" he said.

I said, "That's Greek. Not a common combination," risking the charge of racism that is invoked whenever any comment of any kind is made about ethnicity.

"Not Moussaka—Masaka," a voice behind me said. "M-A-S-A-K-A." A female voice, quiet, clear, *poised*, toneless. "Masaka Kinoshita." The "k"s sounded like tiny nuts being cracked.

I turned. A small person stood in the corridor, not smiling but not unsmiling. A black cap of hair with points curling under her ears, unoccidental eyes, ivory-coloured skin, grey schoolgirl tunic over a white shirt, black shoes. She was loaded down with copy paper.

"Masaka?" I repeated, but without her nutcracker clarity.

"Kinoshita," she repeated, twitching her nose, showing

she was human, distantly related to creatures like me and Ginger, then smiling properly, confirming the twitch came from amusement.

This time, I promised myself, I would get the name straight before sunset, not stumble around with it for two weeks. Masaka Kinoshita. Ma-sa-ka Ki-no-shi-ta. Already in my head, the nuts were starting to crack. "Joe," I said stepping backwards into the table she was heading for, banging my spine against the edge. I grinned and nodded, holding out my hand.

She walked by me, put down the stack of paper, then turned and offered me a tiny ivory paw.

"You're the new sessional," I said.

She smiled again and moved around behind the table, sat down, and drew the stack of paper towards her. It was some kind of questionnaire.

"Masaka's replacing Wanamaker for a few weeks," Ginger said.

Lester Wanamaker was a part-timer who lasted for only three weeks until so many students had come to the department offices to look for him that the chairman decided to make enquiries and learned that Wanamaker had actually only lasted a week before disappearing westwards, back to Saskatchewan, leaving no forwarding address.

We concluded that he had become paralysed with doubt—he had never taught before—because his colleagues, putting together their recollections, found the common thread of his talk had been his worry about where and how to begin, not with the literary material on the course, but with the actual occasion. Should you keep the students waiting so that you could stride in, making an entrance? What should the opening remark be on the first day? Should you stand behind the lectern all the time, or walk about? Should you permit talking in class? And so on.

In any event, according to his students, he had simply walked in with his head down and started to read from the text, "sort of shouting" as one student put it. Sometimes he read a short story, sometimes two. He never looked at them. Towards the end of the week one student asked him what he was doing and he said he was acquainting them with the text.

It was a breakdown, of course; we've seen them before and we should have realised it, so we felt a bit guilty about him.

When he disappeared, some of us did penance by offering to teach a bit of his course, including our chairman, who stays out of the classroom if he can. Now, finally, we had a replacement.

"Have you met a class yet?" I asked Masaka, as I already thought of her, without losing the feeling of weirdness at finding myself the colleague and roommate of Madame Butterfly and realizing why Pinkerton got hooked.

"This will be my first one." She looked at her watch. "At ten," she said.

"What do you plan to do?" I asked.

She took her time, knitting her brows at me slightly, then gave a small shrug. "Teach them," she said, and picked up her stack of paper and left.

chapter six

"Did I say something wrong?" I enquired of Ginger.

"I'd say that your last question was paternalistic, at least, which you might have got away with, but also possibly, to her ear, chauvinistic, and quite likely racist."

"Oh, fuck off. How come?"

"Would you have asked me that on my first day?" He went into a parody of how I looked when I asked the question, leaning forward nearly hunch-backed, open-mouthed, wet-lipped, a soppy smile on my face. "If you had asked me, I'd have told you to stuff it up your jacksie. As she did."

I sighed. I do my best to rid myself of all the prejudices and attitudes I was brought up with, but it's not easy to stop feeling protective when a pretty creature like Masaka flies too close to the flame, and to remember that "protective" these days is spelt "chauvinist".

The door opened. The psychologist across the corridor put his head in. "Hambone," he said.

I was puzzled. This man used to enjoy testing us on literary or grammatical matters—Richard Costril had theorized that he yearned to be regarded as an honorary member of the department—but we had not heard from him for a long time.

Feeling a trick, but having a go anyway, I began "You mean the bone ..."

Ginger cut me off. "Mr. Bones," he said. "A hambone's a white comedian, working in blackface and with an accent like Jack Benny's Rochester. I played the part once in a variety show in grammar school. You couldn't do it now, even in Scunthorpe."

"Who are you?"

I introduced him to Ginger, realizing that probably that was what he wanted.

"Well done," I said to Ginger, when the psychologist had disappeared. "That true?"

"As I sit here," Ginger said. "Now, what do you think of the new roommate." He got up and closed the door.

"You have your eye on her?"

"Don't be silly. I had coffee with her yesterday, when she first arrived."

Why was that silly? Had he finally met a pretty girl he didn't like? She seemed to me a perfect quarry, for him. Me, I am naturally monogamous. I'm not puffed-up about it; maybe it's just that I have a fairly low libido, compared to Ginger, at least. So why was I being silly? Did just asking the question show how silly or naïve I am?

I pondered the possibility that it was obvious to Ginger that Masaka was bespoke, or utterly celibate, or a Japanese nun, and decided that maybe Ginger was just saying that you don't make passes at office mates because of the impossibility, especially for the other office mates, of living an ordinary day-to-day existence afterwards. I said, "You mean it would create an atmosphere?"

He looked at me, then at his hands on the desk, then, in apparent mild despair at his inability to find the language for what was so obvious, looked away from me, waiting for the coin to drop, then said, after another plead-

ing look, "Yes, it would, wouldn't it?" Then he changed
the subject. "You've heard the news?" he asked.

I could tell by the way he lowered his voice and glanced
at the door he didn't mean the news from Beirut or even
Ottawa. Department news, possibly even college news. I
shook my head. "I just walked in," I said. "I saw the
crowds running along the halls, but I just assumed the dam
had broken. No?"

"Sarky fooker," he said. "I'll tell yer: Fred's been made
Dean. We're lewkin' for a new chairman. Temporary, I
would think."

I'm doing my best here to indicate that Ginger slips
into dialect occasionally, especially when he's savouring a
piece of news and wants to put a ribbon round his words.

"What happened to Peer Gynt?"

The dean's name is Peder Gaunt and he's Swedish by
descent not Norwegian, but he had once been nicknamed
Peer Gynt by a sophisticated security guard and it had stuck.
Nobody bore him any malice; it was just a crude mnemonic.

"He's become Associate Vice-President."

"Christ! That makes three of the buggers." When I came
to Hambleton there was just one assistant vice-president;
now there are about ten of them, associates and assistants.

"No, no. He's replacing someone called Sam Coombs."

"Who's become a full vice-president?"

"I understand he's been called to The Buildings. That's
what I heard. 'He's been called to The Buildings,' Nell said."
Nell is the department secretary. "What does that mean?"

"It means the government wants Coombs as an assistant
deputy or some such because the Ministry of Education is
screwing up again. When someone is 'called to The Buildings'
he has to go right away. So we need a new chairman."

"That's reet, laddie," Ginger crowed, his chair legs
crashing down. "Now you've got it. So who shall we have?"

I felt a mild impulse to administer a small snub. Ginger
was a new boy and to put himself eye-to-eye with someone

very much his senior, without asking, was presumptuous, and then I remembered in plenty of time that tenured people felt exactly that way about me. And Ginger was only saying that he and I were equal in one respect: neither of us would get to vote for the new chairman.

"This is going to be fun to watch," I said. "Who is applying?"

"No one so far that I've heard. Who is eligible?"

"Everybody."

"You?"

"No. I'm Nobody, like you, remember?"

"Ah, right."

I had already let Ginger know that within the class system of Hambleton, as in most North American universities, we were the underclass. Our job is to do the same work as the tenured faculty for half the pay. We are "temporary" for the same reason that the drivers of some of the parcel delivery companies are—it makes it easier to fire us. As a result of thirty years of agitation, sessional teachers at Hambleton have quarried out a kind of security by organizing into an association in imitation of the Faculty Association. This has created a kind of permanency for the longer-serving sessionals, like myself, as well as some privileges like the right to use the gym alongside the tenured faculty. The situation is analogous to those unions of black workers that existed in the States at one time, side by side with the white folks.

As I've said, this happens to suit me because I don't have a family to support, and instead of grubbing away on Saturday afternoons in Robarts Library in search of material to help cobble together an article every year, I can read Superman comics if I like.

All this Ginger has now picked up on, but after only six weeks he hasn't had time to get bitter, like Richard Costril his predecessor, or—the word for me is 'philosophical'.

I said, "Klimpt will apply, he always does."

"He seems harmless enough. Is he unpopular, then?"

"Not when he's not running for chairman. But he believes the core of our work should be 'Business Correspondence', and he is silly enough to say so in the interviews. He's not serious, or rather, he's not serious about wanting to teach it; he really wants to warn us that we have to be ready for the day when all the professional faculties will decide to drop English unless it can be shown to be useful like Economics, or Psychology. He says we should keep our eye on the smart cookies in the Philosophy department who are working up a course in 'Business Ethics' to offer to the M.B.A. program. They'll always have work, he says, and we will, too, if we develop an area like 'Correspondence and Report Writing'. So far his colleagues haven't been frightened enough to agree with him."

"Who else?"

"Well, basically, there are two main factions in the department. There are the traditionalists like Bankier and Maisie Potter and Friedman; old hands, trained to teach the texts as if they say what they mean, believing that if you read the thing carefully you can find out what Keats, say, is going on about, and that if you want to bring a dash of psychology or biographical information to bear, you might *overhear* something extra. Most of these people are well into their fifties and don't want to be disturbed, so they will urge one of their own to run. Call them the Blacks.

"In opposition are the 'New Men' and the 'New Women', though some of these are getting a bit long in the tooth, too. These are the people from whom you will hear words like 'deconstruction', 'post-modern', 'structuralism', Derrida, Barthes, and Foucault. I expect for a recent graduate of— where was it? Leeds?—you would find even these terms a bit passé, but we're not in the mainstream and at Hambleton these are the words you will still hear. Call these people the Reds."

"What does it matter if you've got tenure?"

"The Reds can still frighten some of the Blacks. If the new chairman is a Red, then we shall be facing five years of bickering as he attempts to drag the department into the seventies. There was a candidate last time—all this is hearsay, you understand?"

"Stop poncing about. What do you mean 'hearsay'?"

"You know, don't you, that sessional lecturers like us are not eligible to serve on the search committee for the new chairman?"

"No, I didn't know that, no."

"This was something the Faculty Association negotiated. They argued that the temporary staff do not have the same long-term interests as the tenured faculty, so all important matters should be decided by the tenured faculty."

"What are the unimportant matters?"

"As in the old joke, there are no unimportant matters."

"Why? Why don't they give us a look-in?"

"Different reasons in each department. In this one, the two factions I just mentioned are united in their desire to keep out the even newer ideas that sessionals bring with them from the graduate schools. See, the new boys I was talking about are new in the sense that they are the newest, but in this department we haven't hired a full-time person for twenty years, except for Richard Costril. Think of New College, Oxford."

"Do we get any fookin' say in anything? At all?"

"The Faculty Association encourages the tenured staff to consult us informally."

"And do they?"

"Going home on the subway sometimes."

"So when will the politicking start?"

"We seem to have an emergency, so my guess is right away."

At eleven I was in the classroom, teaching the
D.H.Lawrence story "You Touched Me" to an assort-
ment of second year students. I long ago discarded
Lawrence's novels as fevered, over-written, and too long,
but someone put his short story collection, *England, My
England*, on the course and I had learned through these
stories that I was completely wrong. Having failed to
hear what Lawrence was banging on about in the novels,
even in *Lady Chatterley's Lover*, I had assumed that the
fault was his. But these stories blew my mind, took the
top off my head, knocked me out, and left me gasping.
The students liked them, too, or they seemed to.

The thing is, I've boiled the teaching of literature down
to a single question: "Have you noticed this?" That's all. I
chat for a bit, of course, on related matters like what
Lawrence thought of Freud and vice versa, but it all leads
to the point when I ask the question. I'm talking about
allegory, of course, which I've come to believe is what all
teaching of all literature is about. In the case of "You
Touched Me," what I have to offer second year students is
that the story is really the Sleeping Beauty fable, except
that it is the hero who wakes up when touched. There's
even the high hedge around the house/palace. That, plus
the orgy at the end, has students generally agreeing that it
is the best of a very fine collection. They like "Tickets,
Please" too, but "You Touched Me" is a revelation.

I mention this, not by way of a digression, but because
much of the in-fighting in English departments these days
is about literary theory. I have no theory; that is, I do not
think talking about books in a particular way is more valid
than talking about them in some other way, as long as you
are talking about the books and not yourself. But without
the allegory to look for, I'm soon reduced to reading aloud.
And yet I must get this straight: I know that Dickens said
that the function of allegory is to make your head ache,
and I don't think the allegorical approach is better than

any other approach. It is just the one I find most interesting and the most, well, fun. It's the one that can make for lively classroom discussion. Successful teaching of literature consists of keeping the students intrigued by a work long enough that they will go away from the course remembering the words Shakespeare used.

How you do it doesn't matter.

chapter seven

After the class I scuttled back to get another look at Masaka. She was sitting behind her table, reading the index of our first year poetry anthology, choosing and ticking off her choices.

"How did it go?" I asked. It was an unfocussed remark, no more than a "hello" really, and she let me know it.

"How did what go?"

I started to stumble immediately. "The class. It was your first, wasn't it?"

"Here, yes, but I've taught before."

"How did you find them?"

"Who?"

"The students. Our students."

"They're like students," she said, with a quarter of a smile.

"Sorry. I'm just making conversation." In a minute, though, I would get irritated. I *was* just making conversation, just to be agreeable, so why was she doing the inscrutable bit?

But now she increased the smile to half-size. "I thought you might be going to offer me some advice," she said. "Everyone else has, except Ginger. Everyone else wants to explain why Hambleton students are unique. I'd rather find out for myself."

"What did you do with them?"

"Who?"

"The students. The class you just taught."

"I just taught them."

"What?"

"Poetry."

"What am I doing wrong now?"

Now the smile was up to three-quarters. It was slowly filling her face like the blue bit at the bottom of the screen that tells you the computer is loading. I waited, and the blue bit reached the end and the face appeared, smiling on the imaginary desktop I was watching. "I don't know yet," she said. "I'm waiting to find out what you are up to."

Now I had her. "In what way?" I asked.

"In all the usual ways."

"I'm a happily unmarried man, if that's one of the things we are talking about," I said. It was still only eleven in the morning.

"That's one of the things we're talking about. Not the most important."

"Tell me some of the others." This was weird but engrossing. I had known her, after all, for a total of fifteen minutes, and here we were talking as if after an evening of exploration.

"I'll be simple," she said. "Our conversation has consisted entirely of you trying to take me over."

"Me? You? I told you, I'm a happily unmarried man."

"Indeed you are, almost an epigram, aren't you, so I must have meant something else, mustn't I? Think about what you have asked me since you came back to the office."

"I've just been making conversation, making you feel at home. I don't remember all the words I used."

"You've been patronizing me. Would you have asked a forty-year-old male the same questions?'

Just what Ginger had said. Had they been talking?

"Let me think," I began.

To give her credit, she waited while I did.

"First," I said "I'm thirty-five, though I've had a hard life. Second, I think you jumped the gun. As a matter of fact I might have asked an exact male contemporary the same questions out of a spirit of collegiality, a desire to be agreeable to the new man, and a curiosity about how his past experiences had prepared him for his first class at Hambleton, and how our students differed if at all from these experiences. So you might have been totally and utterly wrong.

"However," I held up my hand to stem protest although she hadn't said a word or moved a face muscle to dislodge the set of her smile, "Although you might have been wrong, in fact, you weren't. What I first saw in you this morning was a tyro, someone who might not have taught anywhere before, so my questions certainly flowed out of a patronizing desire to offer warmth and comfort to my new little young female colleague in case the rough engineering students had bruised her.

"Second I saw a Japanese person who I was surprised to hear speak my language so well and I was curious to know if her exotic foreign looks juxtaposed with her obvious command of idiom created a special dynamic in the classroom. Thus on top of patronizing, chauvinistic paternalism, we have to add ethnic stereotyping, and even racism, which, though benevolent—many of my acquaintances are Japanese—is certainly not neutral."

She opened her lips for the first time since I had started my speech. "And third?" she asked. She wasn't being hostile; she was intrigued to see where this was leading. "Third," I said, "is the fact that you're not only young and Japanese, but pretty, so the matter of your being a girl, sorry, a woman, also lay behind my questions. So, yes, I was probably relaxing into my roots and patting the pretty little geisha on the head, wondering, as one does with geishas, when sex would get into the act. I won't do it again."

She got up now and came over to me. I braced for an assault, verbal or one-handed or even a spit in the eye. She leaned over and kissed me on the cheek. "No pats," she said. "Not on the head, or on the bum." She smiled and left the office, moving around Ginger who was standing in the doorway.

"You do something right?" he asked

"I nearly said something wrong. What you saw was her agreeing she might have been over-reacting, and taking the opportunity anyway to let me know where she stood."

"We'll have to be careful, won't we?"

Yes, I thought, we would. Because in spite of Masaka's demonstration that she felt competent to look after herself, I could not believe that her previous experience had included someone like Ginger, and I still felt very protective.

chapter eight

I had no classes until three o'clock so I called Atkinson, my boss at the agency, to log the hours I was spending watching Tyler, then drove into the downtown area and found a place to park near the bookstore.

Across the street, a coffee shop with a ledge under the window and a row of stools gave me a chance to do a bit of surveillance in daylight. I'd never had a good look at Tyler, and I was keen to see inside his store, too. I'd made a few fake enquiries by telephone and established that if I wanted him to look over some books I wanted to sell, I would find him at the store anytime except between twelve and two.

This particular coffee shop makes good sandwiches, and I bought a salmon salad on whole wheat and a coffee, and got myself settled on a stool. Over the top of my newspaper I could watch the door of the bookshop across the street, as well as Tyler's car, which was parked outside.

First, I had to deal with the salmon sandwich, because I had that morning put on a pair of pants just back from the dry cleaners. I took out the lettuce and tomato to eat separately. Then I put a napkin over each half of the sandwich, pressed down firmly, squeezing the surplus salmon mixture out and on to the plate, where I could eat it with my coffee spoon. Now I had a sandwich that was only mouth-thick and wouldn't ooze its filling all over my pants when I tried to eat it.

A headline about a new step in the quest for cloning caught my eye. I allowed the usual thoughts about what Hitler would have made of this bit of science, musing once again on why there had been no reference in the reports to the Czech play, *R.U.R.*, which had predicted the development of cloning and its consequences sixty years ago. I concluded that it was the result of schools of journalism having dropped education from the curriculum and substituting training in information retrieval.

I looked up only just in time to see Tyler standing in his doorway looking up at the sky. He was older than I had guessed from his clothes, which were those of a successful young playwright: authentic-looking tweed Brendan jacket; cream-coloured, thick wool, roll-necked sweater, grey leather trousers; and, red and black trainers. From the neck up, however, he showed the world a creased fifty-ish face set in a small, round head with scanty black hair worn long enough that it had to be making a statement, though I'm not sure what it was saying.

I finished my sandwich as Tyler finished looking at the sky and walked to his car, a yellow Volvo, which, like his costume, defied the observer to guess that its owner was anything as colourless as a book dealer. I ran out the door in time to see him drive over to Spadina and turn right. I crossed the street and walked into his shop.

The little bell above the door pinged, causing the young man sorting a pile of books to look up, and just as quickly, to look away to avoid eye contact. He would have been out of place anywhere else, but he did have just the look of an antique book dealer's very underpaid assistant; someone who wanted no part of the world out there, wanted only to be left to handle books in silence. When I spoke to him he looked to the left and right of the pile of books, seeking a way to respond without looking up. I felt like an unwanted prison visitor. In response to my question, "May I look around?" he jerked his head up sharply and allowed it to sink slowly to a position of rest as if he never quite got the signal right. Then he ignored me, though I think he sneaked a quick look as I turned away.

The store was typical, thousands of books, many unreadable and unsaleable (*Statutes of Ontario: 1898*), grouped in categories on old warehouse shelving from floor to ceiling. The shelves were so close that a fat antiquarian would block the aisle, the upper shelves were out of reach, the whole the result of turning an old house into a mine of books complete with dimly lit tunnels.

I sidled along the rows for ten minutes, wondering professionally if there were any security cameras, and if there was any chance of finding a valuable book the owner hadn't recognized. ("... it's a first edition. There are only eleven known copies. I found it in the twenty-five cent bin outside a bookseller on College.") I wondered, too, what sort of living it was; as with all those stores, all the time I was there only one other person walked in, and he left without buying anything. But rent had to be paid, surely, and some sort of wages to the furtive young gent behind the counter, though he didn't look as if he needed much. I considered the owner's not-cheap threads, though, and his fairly recent Volvo, and wondered if the store was a front. Front for what? Stolen antique books? Could you launder thug money through a second-hand bookstore?

I followed the tunnel of books to the back of the room where what was probably a fireplace in the corner had been boarded up and fronted with more shelving. In the other corner, a narrow flight of bare wooden stairs led me to a second floor with what I took to be a whimsical sign over the doorway, "Dollar Store"—a way of saying this was the cheap section of the second-hand paperback area, mainly crime fiction and romance.

The bell pinged downstairs. I looked out the window and saw the yellow Volvo outside again; Tyler was back, had probably forgotten something. I heard him speaking to the assistant whose replies were inaudible, then the bell pinged again and Tyler re-emerged on to the street and drove off. I picked up a copy of *The Old Dick* by L.R. Morse, a much under-appreciated novel I was always glad to pick up as a stocking-stuffer for people who hadn't heard of it, and took it down to the desk with my dollar. "Did you see the yellow Volvo?" I asked him, cheerily, companionably. "Nice car."

He put the book in an old paper bag and took my dollar.

"One of your customers?" I asked.

He raised his eyebrows. "The owner," he whispered, looking down again at whatever he was working at.

"You're not the owner?" I asked, amazed.

He blinked, looked around his desk, said, "No," and waited for me to go away.

Where do the proprietors of used bookstores find them?

chapter nine

B ack at the college, I called in on Bert Tensor, the department bibliophile. Bert likes books; books as objects, I
mean, not just as reading matter. Myself, I have a few hundred books which indicate what I do for a living—some texts
I was assigned as an undergraduate, all of Graham Greene,
Evelyn Waugh, George Orwell, William Trevor—these are
the books I keep to reread while crossing the Atlantic at
night. I don't collect books, I don't hoard the ones I get, and
I have managed to get past the desire to ivy-league my office
with them. What the students make of the empty bookcases
behind me I don't know, probably nothing.

Bert Tensor is the opposite of me in every way. He still
has every book he has ever bought; his office and most of
the rooms in his house, including the basement, are lined
with books he keeps moist and claims to have read, or
looked at. He certainly knows if he owns a book, the real
test of a bibliophile.

On Saturday afternoons he is released from the house
and kids for three hours by his wife to prowl the second-
hand bookshops, on his own. In exchange, he looks after
the kids on Sunday afternoons while she looks at houses
that are for sale. He is the only member of the department

whose book collection is distinct from his profession of teaching literature. The rest of us play tennis or watch baseball or garden, or even repaint our bathrooms, but Bert's hobby is books, and in the course of pursuing his hobby he has become the department's expert resource.

"Jason Tyler," I said. "He has a bookshop on College Street."

"I know Tyler," he said. "What do you want to know about him?"

"Whatever you know. Is he shady? Squeaky clean? An expert in any field? Most of all, what kind of person is he? His, whatdoyoucallit, character?"

"I haven't cultivated his acquaintance. I don't like him, his stock isn't very interesting, and it doesn't change much."

"You know anything about his personal life?"

"No."

"Why don't you like him?"

"No good reason, just an immediate instinctive antipathy. If I knew him I might like him, but I don't want to know him. And don't ask me why." He made a face to keep the remark airy.

"But you don't know of anything dishonest, disreputable?"

"No, I told you. Now if you'd ask me about his predecessor in that store I could tell you a story."

"Tell me anyway. How long has Tyler been the owner?"

"Two years, maybe. A bit less. Not long, anyway. I used to go in all the time when James Curry owned it. I haven't been in twice since it changed hands. The last time a woman in there asked me if she could help me. I said I was just browsing. She asked me for what, maybe she could point me in the right direction. I never went back."

"Why?"

"A salesperson coming on strong in an antiquarian bookshop, even one as tatty as Tyler's?"

"Well, it *is* a shop," I reminded him.

"So it is." He gave up on me as one of the people who could not differentiate between a bookshop and a used car lot, and went back to his reading. I said, "So tell me about James Curry."

Tensor searched the air for the name. "Huh?"

"The story about the predecessor."

He laid his book aside and prepared to get rid of me. "Here's a story, then. Once upon a time someone left a valuable manuscript with Curry to evaluate, and Curry lost it. He said it was stolen, along with some other odds and ends, but it never turned up in the trade. I think that the owner of the manuscript threatened to assault him. But the manuscript was never recovered."

"What was it a manuscript of?"

"One of the moderns."

By "moderns" Tensor means anybody after Beaumont and Fletcher. "Which one?"

"The one who worked for the newspaper."

"Christ. Hemingway?"

"Hemingway. Yes, that sounds like it." Tensor gave a small smile to show he was teasing, but I know he doesn't think much of Hemingway. He was shrinking him by affecting to have barely heard the name.

I said, "There's a story about Hemingway and the *Toronto Star*, isn't there?"

"You see? You already know it. Is that it, then?" He picked up his book.

"Was the theft news at the time? When was this? What was it the manuscript of?"

Tensor said, "Some poems, I think. Did he write poetry? He did, didn't he? Awful doggerel." He grinned to show he was only playing about, then leaned forward, the body language of engagement and seriousness. "I think it must have been news or I wouldn't have heard of it. I don't read newspapers, and I don't remember Curry saying anything. I probably heard it on one of those three-minute

Arts programs the CBC puts on before the real news. When was it? About twenty years ago, not long after I joined the department, because I didn't know Curry well enough for him to have chatted to me about it. As I remember, the manuscript wasn't the beginning of a book but a collection of drafts of stories that Hemingway had saved, knowing he would be famous one day, the way writers these days save up their drafts in the hope of one day persuading a library to buy them."

"That's your story about Curry?" I asked after waiting for more.

"What kind of story are you after? I'll tell you another one, a human interest story. Curry never answered the phone."

"Why did he bother to have a phone at all if he didn't answer it?"

"So that his address could be listed in the phone book, the Yellow Pages. And to be able to call out to get Swiss Chalet to deliver. And some of the messages were important; they just weren't urgent."

"But what if they *were* urgent. Some must have been."

"Try keeping a diary. How many life-or-death messages do you get? People adjusted to him. They gave him a day to answer his machine. Very occasionally, a friend would want to let him know that a book he was interested was available if he were quick, then they used a courier. Curry said couriers were today's version of the telegrams the Bloomsbury crowd used to invite each other to tea with."

This wasn't fascinating, but it had given me a chance to think. "Do you think there really was a Hemingway manuscript?"

"Papers; not manuscript, papers. Oh, yes."

"What do you think happened?"

"I think they were stolen. Not by Curry, I should say. For an antiquarian bookseller, Curry was very honest." He looked at his watch. "And that's all I know about Mr. Hemingway's papers. Perhaps you should talk to David."

"He told me the story once."

"Make him do it again."

chapter ten

The story of Hemingway's stay in Toronto is part of the city's folklore. Hemingway worked as a reporter for the *Toronto Daily Star* for a few months before he went to Paris and became the paper's European correspondent. He discovered that his stint as a reporter had given him his style, and sat down to write "Up in Michigan".

At one time all Canadian undergraduates registered in English knew the story of Hemingway's residency in Toronto, and graduate students from Saskatchewan still sometimes pay a visit to the Selby Hotel on Sherbourne Street to raise a glass in the tavern of the hotel where he stayed, and students doing an M.A. in American literature also visit the other places where he slept—on Bathurst Street and Lyndhurst Avenue—if only to avoid being tripped up on their oral.

Somehow I missed hearing the story in graduate school, but as soon as I arrived at Hambleton College it was told to me by David Wintergreen, a specialist in American Literature. Actually, David is now drifting sideways out of American literature into poetry (his own)—something that often happens to senior academics a few years before they retire. In David's case, he is also drifting backwards into a kind of literary criticism which the periodicals he submits articles to will not take seriously, believing *he* is not serious. I think he is.

David's thesis is that much literary writing is affected by technical problems that the writer has to get around. Searching for the meaning of a text in the author's life, in his or her society, in myth and archetypes, in psychology, is all very well, but before you decide any question of meaning you need to be sure that you have understood the possible reasons why a text is thus and not thus.

David was put on to this by reflecting on his own practices when writing, in the days when he had abandoned research and was looking about for something to do in the three or four days a week left from his teaching schedule, before he took up verse. Back then, before word processors, the skill and energy of the typist would often affect the text of a story, between drafts especially. Narratives would be changed by the need to correct a blunder in such a way that it would not be necessary to retype the next thirty pages. Something had to be done on page eight of the second draft and perhaps to page nine, to make them final so the rest of the typescript could be left as it was. Thinking about copy typists and their like, all the way back to the monks with their dirty habits, copying the word in their cells, David believed he had discovered his life's work.

Once attuned, he found examples in everything he taught—we all contributed suggestions—and he is currently applying for a Canada Council grant to get the time to work up a paper on the topic. In the course of his enquiries, David stumbled across the case of Jake Barnes, the impotent hero of *The Sun Also Rises*, a case which David saw as a valid extension of his own method.

When preparing a lecture on the novel, he saw that all the usual explanations of Jake's impotence were beside the point. What he found in the learned journals was that the literary meaning, the symbolism of Jake's problem, though endlessly and variously teased out, was first of all seen as essentially personal, representing Jake's inability after his war-time experiences to find meaning in the universe (this view is often supported by quoting from a passage in *A Farewell to Arms*, a tragic love story written several years later). Secondly, and universally, was the inability of the world to replace the loss of faith brought on by the failure of the war to end wars. Nada.

It is David's contention that all this is no more than elegant chat, a collection of verbal constructs spun out of the critics' bowels. The real point is that Barnes is impotent because Hemingway at the time decided that impotency was one of the few ways left in which sex, especially the sex act, could be made interesting on paper. Thus Hemingway, needing a love story, and unable to believe that anyone could still render the climactic act interesting, rendered it impossible, because *that* was interesting. Departments of English had been searching for a symbolic understanding of what was only a technical difficulty. (Wintergreen, by the way, also allows for the possibility that Hemingway's age had something to do with it. Impotence, Wintergreen speculates, might have been a good literary idea to the youngish writer of *The Sun Also Rises*, but to the mature writer of *A Farewell to Arms*, it was something to be feared.)

Finally, David wonders if the idea of impotence came to him one day during the act, as it were, while he was making mental notes as to how he would describe it in his novel and thinking about it so deeply that it took his mind off the act and, bingo, the idea of impotence was sprung. But this is mere speculation and no use in a serious academic discussion.

Wintergreen is very deeply read, in Hemingway and elsewhere, as he searches for the solutions writers have employed to solve the day-to-day problems of their trade, and he was able to supply me with everything I needed to know.

"The hotel Hemingway stayed in was the Selby," he said, "But the one you want is the Garrick, about half a block south on the other side."

I waited.

"It's something that often gets muddled in the printed accounts. The point is that the manuscripts, the papers, whatever, were found in a renovation of a hotel that is not connected to Hemingway at all. How did they get there?" He placed his fingertips together.

"David. I'm not a seminar. Just tell me. Surely someone like you has tried to find out."

"Sorry. Yes. No. So far no one has cared enough to find out. I'm keeping my eye on it, of course, and if you come across anything, let me know.

"The two hotels have become one in the accounts I've read, always called the Selby, but that isn't where the papers were found. Point is, we *know* where Hemingway was every day of his stay in Toronto, so no one cares that seventy years later some papers surfaced at the Garrick, then disappeared. If they reappeared, it wouldn't matter where they were found, as long as they were authentic.

"I think it's interesting. It may be that the papers were, in fact, discovered at the Selby by a workman who was painting one of the bedrooms, and discarded or forgotten at the Garrick when the workman was on the next job. Another theory involves a prostitute—the Garrick was part brothel—and there are plenty of others. But the speculation, never very strong once the papers disappeared, died out.

"Nowadays the biographies don't even mention the Garrick, and a casual mention of "the Hemingway Papers" generally refers to another set lost on a French train. And now they've found a whole new batch in Hemingway's old basement in Cuba, but if I were you and wanted to find out whose hands were last on the *Toronto* Hemingway papers, I wouldn't bother with the Selby yet. Think Garrick."

chapter eleven

It was Carole's turn to cook so we had the thawed three-month-old remains of a carton of arrabiata sauce from Pusiteri's poured over spaghettini with some grated parmesan, a salad from the bin of pre-washed green stuff in Loblaws, the heel of a loaf of Italian bread from Spiga's (the best bread in Toronto),and a bit of Stilton with Carr's water biscuits, all washed down with the dregs of a bottle of Penascal, a Spanish wine we buy by the case and will continue to do so as long as the LCBO continues to stock it.

I go into such brand name detail only to show how well we live considering how much Carole dislikes cooking. It's not that she can't cook, it's just that it interferes with the six or eight hours a day she sets aside for reading. I, on the other hand, like the idea of cooking; I'm just no good at it. I have no instinct for it, and too often when I am following a recipe I concentrate so hard that I can't remember where I'm at and omit or double the quantity of some spice like cayenne with the result that the dish withers the taste buds or turns into baby food. So nowadays, when it's my turn, like Carole, I tend to rely on whatever Pusiteri's or Ziggy's has cooked and I can take home to warm up. The task has lately been made more difficult by the disappearance of Marks and Spencers, at one time the purveyors of the most edible instant food in town. As back-up we buy assorted spaghetti sauces from Pusiteri's, six cartons at a time. Though I have no talent for the stove, I have developed three company dishes that even I can't screw up, three dishes that I now cook in rotation whenever we have guests. We entertain so rarely that these three should see me out.

Carole said, "How's Ginger?"

Ginger and Carole like each other. They communicate on some wavelength outside my range. Nothing to do with sex, I'm sure. When I brought him home for dinner she sensed almost immediately that Ginger was sexually audacious, and successful, but when the two of them locked over the dining-table it was because of something else they found in each other. When he was gone, I asked Carole what women saw in him, and she said she hadn't the faintest idea. She thought perhaps he had something that he switched off in our house as a courtesy to me, but said I could bring him to dinner whenever I liked because he was one of the select group of people (two or three) who were as interesting as the book she was currently reading. Then, mind-reading, she said, as she had said once or twice before over the years of our relationship, "Don't worry. It's you I love."

I said, "Thanks. But back to Ginger. I think I may have a problem."

"As a roommate?"

"Sort of. I don't know how it didn't come up at dinner, but we have another roommate."

"And they might not get along? Something like that?" Carole looked at her watch and hung on to her book.

"I'm afraid they'll get along very well. Our new roommate is female, Japanese and luscious."

"Says you?"

"Objectively. She just is. You can't avoid seeing it, and thinking it. I'm afraid that I'm going to have to knock on the door when I come back from class."

"Don't be silly." She looked up from her book and focused on me. "Bring her home."

"Here? I thought feeding Ginger was our quota for this term."

"I didn't mean for dinner, but okay, if you like." She thought about this for a moment. "No," she said. "Not for dinner. She might be a vegetarian, hard to feed. Make it brunch on a Sunday. And ask Ginger again. We could have bagels and lox and salad with bean sprouts, something for everybody. Oh, hell, whatever you think. No, Friday for dinner."

I assumed in spite of what she said that Carole's behaviour was her way of finding out if her territory—me—was likely to be invaded. As I say, except for her sister and brother-in-law, we almost never feed people. I felt quite chuffed, a word Ginger taught me. He says it means elated.

Next morning I typed up my report on the book dealer and faxed it to the agency on Carole's machine. I waited for a few minutes, then called the agency. I wanted to confirm my orders, because now we had established what her husband was doing I wanted to know if she wanted me to carry on. I never thought I'd be involved in taking pictures of bare-assed adulterers since none of that is really necessary for a divorce. Now, as I've said, if you want out, you just hire a shark and get him to negotiate the best deal he can for you. A wise man or woman draws up the divorce settlement before the wedding even if it casts a cloud over the nuptials.

This woman didn't need any more evidence than she had, as far as I knew, so I asked the boss if that was that, now that I had recorded two assignations, but he called me back and said she wanted me to carry on until further notice. The one new order I got was that she would like a picture of the woman, or rather two pictures, taken on different days, and I was to be careful to date the pictures, which I thought was a little strange. All I could think of was that Mrs. Tyler wanted to make sure that it was the same woman all the time in case Tyler was insatiable and diddling every woman who browsed the Biography shelves. But it was none of my business, and I always need the money.

chapter twelve

The news along the Rialto was all of the soon-to-be-vacant department chair. Before I reached the office I was waylaid in the cafeteria by Richard Costril, my old comrade-in-arms, now an establishment fink. Richard began, "You heard about Fred?"

I said, "Heard what?"

"He's quitting. We're looking for a new chair."

"*You* are," I corrected him. "I shall do as I'm told, whoever is in charge."

I wasn't being caustic. Richard had long been the angriest man in the college, suffering like the rest of us, only now released by a set of circumstances that would have provided the plot for a Gilbert and Sullivan opera, and thus in another space from me. I wished him luck but I saw no reason to help him feel comfortable. As far as I was concerned there was enough comfort for him in his newly accessed pension plan.

"I need somebody to talk to," he said.

"Then I'm no use to you. I'm nobody."

"Oh, for Christ's sake. You've been teaching *The Odyssey* for too long. Look, I have to talk to you. I need to think my way through this. Any day now they'll be forming a committee to choose the new man and I will have to vote."

"Surely the committee will do that? You elect a committee and they recommend someone. Isn't that how it works? That's what I heard. Maybe just hearsay, below-stairs gossip."

"That's how it used to be. But some of them are alarmed at what they see as the possible outcome and they're canvassing me."

"You mean they might not get their choice? That's bound to happen to some of them, surely. It's called the committee system, or democracy, in academe."

I was enjoying myself. Having no power, I also didn't suffer from not getting my way in departmental affairs, whereas the tenured faculty was more or less permanently seething as the factions tried to get control.

"I'm being courted," Richard repeated. "They all want me on their side, but so far they don't know if I'm available; they don't know where I stand on anything."

"Hoist with their own petard," I said.

"What?"

"Because they had to give you tenure to shut you up, they didn't interview you properly so they don't know what you think about anything."

"No, nor do I. That's why I need you. Fact is," he giggled, "I rather enjoy being an enigma." He made a 'Who me?' face, a parody of an enigmatic look. "But I need your help. I need someone to talk with about the possibilities, someone who knows them, who overhears them in their unguarded moments, but who is himself objective."

To his credit he blushed a little at this blatant flattery, but I let him off lightly. "Gossip from the servants' hall, you mean," I said. "We hear everything. We're invisible."

"When can we get together?"

"I have classes. Let's say, three, for coffee, here?"

"Make it the Second Cup on the corner."

"Right. I'll act surprised when you appear. 'Richard!' I'll cry. 'How's it going up there on Olympus? How are you getting along with Zeus? I hear he wants out.'"

"Oh, fuck off. Three-fifteen then."

"You paying? See, on my salary ..."

"Give it a rest, will you?"

"My partner would like you both to come to dinner," I said. "On Friday, if possible."

I made the announcement as soon as I arrived at the office and found Ginger and Masaka there, working. On the drive along Eastern Avenue I had debated with myself how to approach it. If I asked them separately, then I might get a 'yes' from Ginger and a 'no' from Masaka, and the idea was for Carole to get a look at Masaka. She'd already met Ginger. I also felt I had to let them know what they were in for, and their answers might depend in each case on the awareness that the other had been invited, too.

Ginger said, "What's with this *partner* lingo, Joe? You gay? Coming out?"

This wasn't just flippant banter. As Ginger spoke he was looking back and forth between Masaka and me for some reason. He seemed to be sending her a message, though I couldn't figure out what it might be. Perhaps just clarifying what 'partner' meant in my case.

I said to Masaka, "My partner's name is Carole with an 'e'. She works as a translator and speechwriter, mainly for the government. Just an old-fashioned unmarried couple, I'm afraid. Ginger has met Carole; he's just being facetious."

Masaka said, "I'll be very pleased. What time?"

"Seven. If you want to bring someone ..."

Ginger looked up. Masaka said, "Just him," pointing to Ginger, apparently playfully. Her expression did not change.

"Carole also asked me to ask about the menu."

"Tops is pie and chips," Ginger said. "But I can eat anything except pumpkin pie. Problem 'nnit, feeding a Jap and a Limey? What about you, Masaka?"

"I can eat anything except liver."

"I'll have hers," Ginger said.

So that was that.

chapter thirteen

The next class was one I never looked forward to. Some previous instructor had put together a course in creative writing and then died; the students had already registered and none of the tenured people wanted it, so I was stuck with it. When I enquired what I was supposed to do, I was told that it was the kind of course that flowed (that was actually the word used) from the individual instructor's view of the creative process. In other words, I had to make something up.

I read several books on the subject all of which talked a great deal. Some even had exercises at the back, but what they didn't provide was faith, the thing I lacked. When I tried to prepare to teach the substance of what seemed the best-written book on the subject, it fell to pieces in my hands. It was just chat.

I got very frightened and I have stayed that way, stumbling along, waiting for the students to find out I don't know what I'm doing. Somebody explained the idea of "workshopping", and it seemed like the answer, but in my hands the discussion stays at such a low level that I am afraid one of my colleagues will overhear ("What did you think of Emily's opening paragraph, speaking as a mother, Cynthia?"

"You agree, Cyril?"). As far as possible I try not to comment myself in case they find out I have nothing to say.

Otherwise I tell myself that I didn't choose to teach the bloody course, and if there is a spark of talent anywhere in the room I am no more likely to extinguish it than anyone else. In the meantime, we go on, week after week with an ever-diminishing number of students as one after the other they drop out a day or two before their turn in the barrel.

Today we are to hear a story by an old woman with straw in her hair, who lives alone in the woods. That is how she described herself at the beginning of the term when the students were introducing themselves. "I am an old woman who lives alone in the woods," she said, and closed her eyes.

She is one of the extramural students the dean shoehorns into the regular classes to make a little extra money for the college. As a senior citizen, she can take any college course she likes, free (we collect from the government, of course), and you often find one of them in the corner of the room at the beginning of term. When I looked up her records, it turned out that she lives on Ward's Island in the Toronto harbour among far too many ordinary people to be a genuine hermit. She is in her mid-seventies, I think, dressed in homemade-looking clothes with a great fan of frizzy hair in which she sometimes sticks dried flowers, hence the straw that is left behind when she removes them. It is the flowers, I think, that give her a musty smell, as of an old empty barn.

I have no idea what to expect. Two years ago I had an old man in the classroom when I was teaching a course on Romanticism to Journalism students. He sat in the back corner and watched me for a month, while I taught Wordsworth. When I moved on to Coleridge, he shifted towards the middle of the class, and then, the day I was to introduce "The Ancient Mariner" he was sitting in the front row.

I began with a flourish, not opening the text but intoning the first stanza from memory as I sorted out my lecture notes—"It is an ancient Mariner, / And he stoppeth one of three, etc."—to show that today at least I had something in mind by way of a prepared lecture.

I paused and opened the text, but the voice of the ancient mariner continued, as my old student went on, reciting the whole of the first part while the other students listened and I tried to think of a way to contain him. But that was what he came for, to recite the poem, and to show he could. I managed some remarks at the end of his performance, and let the class go early. He waited for me, as if I had asked him to, and then began to answer the question I hadn't asked.

"I first heard it as a kid," he said. "On the corner of Yonge and Dundas in the Depression. There was a lad who used to recite it, you know, a beggar. Then once, I was in a bar in San Francisco and there was a bunch of veterans talking and one of them said, '*The many men so beautiful! / And they all dead did lie: / And a thousand thousand slimy things / Lived on; and so did I*' This was after Vietnam. I set about learning the whole poem, then."

"All seven parts?"

"Oh, yes."

He looked contented as he left the room, and he never came back.

So you never know what a senior citizen is going to surprise you with.

A story about cats as people, that's what we got; a sort of feline *Animal Farm*. It started with a bit of stuff about a cat named Periwinkle who lived with an old woman in the woods, and at that point I suspect I looked like Woody

Allen watching a ballet, but then night fell (in the story) and all the cats came out of their houses and tried to kill each other. That is, a whole new world appeared, a very bad one, an allegory, I guess, of her daytime existence.

I'm going to have to fudge my response until I've read the script; the other students were stunned or appalled, I couldn't tell which, but she'd certainly made something happen, and I don't think her story was intended for children.

And that's the other trouble with Creative Writing: when something remarkable is read, maybe once every two years, half of it goes by before you realise that this time something is really happening. Thank God for the bell, and the chance to come back at it.

chapter fourteen

Richard waited for me at the Second Cup, as promised. He started in immediately. "It looks like we are going to get four candidates," he said. "And the department as a whole is going to function as the selection committee. They are going to draw up a short list to interview, and we'll all go to the interview, except the people in your room, of course, then we'll vote. The department is about evenly split, if I've counted right."

"Between?"

"Oh, you know. The Reds and the Blacks. Between those who haven't read any criticism since 1960 and those who stopped reading in 1980. The Reds, the new men, represented by Scopp and Jenkins, and the Blacks, the traditionalists, led by either Daniels or Johnson."

"Put me down as one of those, a traditionalist."

"You're a bit of a borderline case. Some of the Blacks suspect you."

"Of what? Being a closet post-structuralist?"

"You do make them uneasy. They don't understand why someone of your age and lack of qualifications is content to roll along, year after year, without finishing his thesis or publishing anything."

"Why do they care? They need me to do their teaching."

"They get uneasy when someone shakes the tree. It's like "The Lottery", the Shirley Jackson story. There are rumours that folks in the next village are doing away with tenure."

I laughed. "Just as you've finally got it. So what's this to do with me?"

"You look like someone who doesn't care about the present because he knows a thing or two about the future. They'd like to know what you're thinking in case the rules change and you get a vote."

"On what?"

"On anything. As the most senior temporary faculty member, you are seen as someone who must be carrying a gigantic grudge against them, a natural leader capable of heading the revolt when it comes."

"Tell them to leave me out of their worries. Tell them I'm writing a novel."

"Are you?"

"Of course. Isn't everyone around here? But it's slow work so I have no time for politics. Now tell me what's happening."

"Okay. Now, the Blacks are divided. That is, some of the Blacks want Johnson and some want Daniels."

"But they are both Black, aren't they? What's the difference?"

"They've both been chairman before, so we know their true colours. Johnson is a meddler, likes to change things, never anything important, but it's irritating."

"Daniels, then?"

"Not that simple. Daniels is only interested in the chairman's job to reduce his teaching load. Last time he got it down to one two-hour seminar a week. Even his friends thought that was a bit much."

"Is he that lazy?"

"Not lazy; he just hates the classroom. But he does

leave us alone and I think he'll probably get the nod over Johnson."

"And the Reds?"

"It looks like John Jenkins."

"Who else will there be? Any non-aligned independents, maybe?"

"Rumour has offered two others."

"They are?"

"Maurice Riddell."

"*Riddell*? You're surely taking the piss, as Ginger would say."

He held up his hand in case I was launched into full-scale jeering.

Riddell is the department recluse. Originally from Belfast with a Ph.D from somewhere in the American mid-west, he says almost nothing in public. In department meetings he seems to wait until a vote is required, and even then if it is clear his vote will make no difference, he leaves without casting it.

Through sheer seniority he teaches the courses he prefers, though oddly not necessarily the ones that others want. One that includes both *Crime and Punishment* and *Moby Dick*, for example, left behind by a long-gone colleague, a course which frightens the life out of the rest of us; another course on "Classics in Translation", offered to Journalism students, for which he has taken the trouble to brush up his high school Latin and learn what he called "a few words" of Greek. Again, it's a course that would not come readily to hand for the rest of us. As well as these he teaches two sections of the general courses that we all have to be ready to teach, offered to first- and second-year students, and thus he has accepted three hours more than the rest of his tenured colleagues.

Politically, in all the arenas where the adverb might be applied, no one has any idea where he stands. He avoids us as far as possible, or seems to. He arrives at his office, changes into his teaching costume—a polo-necked sweater (he has several in different colours), chinos, and trainers. He teaches his classes, and leaves.

Again, unlike the rest of us, he never takes a teaching problem to a colleague, not even when he is teaching something for the first time. ("What the hell do you *do* with this" is most commonly heard at the beginning of the year when the faculty face their new courses. The famous witticism, "Have I read it? I haven't even *taught* it yet," which was believed to have been coined at the University of Manitoba one September, can still be heard when the term begins.)

Chairmen who want to know what Riddell is doing find themselves unable to get their foot in the door. When asked, he repeats the course outline; questioned about assignments, he offers the sheet he distributes to his students at the beginning of the term, a formidable document that intimidates the rest of us into retyping our own outlines.

Students come out of his office looking lighter, as if they have been to confession. No student ever complains about him. It is as if they are in league with him, protecting him from the rest of us. Fred, the chairman whom we are losing, told a colleague (from whom the story entered the department lore) that he had once tackled a student as he was leaving Riddell's office and called him into his own office to ask him exactly what he was getting out of Riddell's course. (Fred pretended he was doing a survey).

"A great deal," the student said.

"In what way?" Fred asked.

"In every way," the student said, now making it clear that he considered the question impertinent and irrelevant. Fred was reported to have said afterwards, "I felt I was questioning an acolyte about his master's secrets."

Finally, Fred devised a way to peek at the results of Riddell's teaching, and asked Riddell if he would mind if someone else marked a batch of his end-of-term exams.

"Of course not," Riddell said. "Whose will I get to mark?"

That was the end of that because when the idea was made clear to the department, no one was willing to let a stranger see a set of his own papers in exchange for a look at Riddell's.

There has never been the smallest suggestion of the various kinds of creepiness that accompany an unordinary relationship between an instructor and his class; it leaves only the possibility that Riddell is a great teacher with an untroubled understanding of his subject which he can communicate with ease, and without any help from his colleagues. It is hard to believe, but the possibility makes the chairmen wary. One of the Reds managed to formulate an objection to Riddell's "Classics in Translation" course: he said that he felt it lacked theory (those were his words) but did not feel he could challenge Riddell personally. "That's the chairman's job," he said.

Now Richard Costril said, "He threw his hat in the ring after the last department meeting. The dean came to the meeting to urge us to speed up the process of selecting a new chairman, and at the end he wanted to know why there were so few candidates. Then he asked a couple of people at random why they weren't applying. Dewhurst said it had never crossed his mind; when the dean asked Maurice Riddell, Maurice said the same. Then the dean said, "Well, now that it has, will you apply?" and Riddell said all right, and that was that. Maurice left before we could ask him if he meant it, but by this morning Dick had established that he did."

"What does he stand for? Does he have plans?"

"I gather we'll find out at the interview."

"Will you put yourself forward for chair of the committee?"

"Er—no," he said, emphasising the "er", as if mocking the suggestion.

I picked up on the fake hesitation, as I was supposed to. "Why?"

He waited for me to guess, then said, "Because I am the fourth candidate."

"For chairman! But you've only been respectable for a year!"

"I spent a long time waiting."

"But have you thought about it much? What do you have in mind for the job? I mean, what will your platform be?" "Healing," he said, like a Sunday morning television therapist, unctuousness making his face shiny. "Bringing together the warring factions. Stanching the blood from the open wounds. I believe I'm well placed to bring a new health to the department."

"You're the biggest shit-disturber the department has ever had." I was fairly sure he was not expecting me to take him seriously, but I had to provoke him to admit it. "Until you got tenure."

He laughed and struck a pose like an old-time politician. "I've fought the good fight more than once, yes, but now I'm ready to set that all aside, to answer the call, and to shoulder the burden of peacemaker."

"You won't do it with clichés. So what are we here for? You and me? Here. Now."

"I want you to be a conduit for me. Everyone still links us closely because of our years together in the trenches …"

"Knock it off, Richard."

"What?"

"This 'years together in the trenches' bullshit. Jargon, slogans, electioneering. Don't talk like that to me."

I still wasn't sure what Richard was up to. He was making fun of the role he would have to play, certainly, but I felt some slight hardening of the arteries in his speech and I wanted to protect myself against any change in him that might affect me. "I'll tell you what I'll do, Richard. I'll be a conduit, a real one. You tell me what you want known, about yourself and your plans, and I'll tell everybody else in confidence. At the same time I'll tell you everything I hear from others about their opinions of your what-shall-I-call-it?—run for office? In other words, I'll tell everybody, including you, everything I know or hear. No one will believe that I don't have a private agenda, I'll make sure of that; they'll know I'm up to something, and I'll be known as the Machiavelli of Hambleton. It'll be fun. Are you really serious, by the way?"

I just slipped that last question in to see if I could catch him in an automatic honest response. No luck.

"I think I have something to offer the department ..."

"Don't start that again. I mean do you really want the job, never mind the bullshit?"

"Yes, I do."

"That's the first thing I'll tell them, then, in case they think you're just shit-disturbing again."

The poor fool didn't have a hope, but I didn't say anything. He'd caught a sniff of the barmaid's apron and it had gone straight to his head.

So I was committed to pass on everything I heard; but not everything I thought.

chapter fifteen

A week later I was parked opposite Tyler's room, observing the usual shenanigans.

I had followed Tyler from the bookstore to Harbord Street, watched the lights go on, the blind being pulled down, the silhouettes merging into an embrace, the lights go out, the period of darkness — a little longer this time — then the lights switched on, the silhouettes' final embrace, then final darkness and in due time Tyler and his lady emerged from the side door and separated after a final more-than-goodnight kiss. I stayed with the lady because I had to get some kind of picture of her. I'm not much of a cameraman — actually, I'm nothing of a cameraman — but the boss had given me a little lesson in pointing and shooting and I hoped that in a strong street light I might catch enough of an image to satisfy the client. If the lady had walked with a limp, or dyed her hair pink, then identifying her to a client might have been easier, but she was simply rather taller than average, blonde, not thin, but not fat; more Renoir than Rubens.

I followed her to her car, a basic Honda, parked not far behind mine, and we drove together up Spadina and over to a small house on Albany, not all that far from the apartment I shared with Carole. She locked the car and walked about ten yards along Albany, before turning into the front yard of a house. I couldn't get a picture because the light was poor and most of the time she was hurrying with her back to me. But I got an idea.

The next morning I left home early and parked on Albany not far from her car. I hoped if she drove to work, whenever that was, I would be able to get a picture in daylight, snapping her profile from inside my car, getting a good enough image to satisfy the client.

I spent four hours sitting in the car waiting for her, wondering if she was taking a day off from whatever she did for a living. I had to move a couple of times because if you sit in a car for that long in any inhabited spot in Toronto, an old lady who sits in her window all day, watching, will call the cops.

Finally, around noon, her door opened and she trotted out and I got her in focus, but she had forgotten something and went back inside and when she re-emerged she was running too fast for me to catch her on film. She stepped quickly into her little car as I climbed into mine and we turned along Dupont, then south on St. George and on to Beverley all the way to Queen, where she dumped the car in the parking lot on the corner and headed, still running, along to Le Clochard, and disappeared inside the restaurant. I found a parking space on the street, wondering if her route was really faster than coming down Spadina. As I fed my two dollars into the dispenser and collected the ticket, I was able to watch her re-emerge with an apron on and with a bundle of the cutlery that she needed to set up lunch up on the sidewalk tables. I got an idea for my next move. I would be illustrating a story for a magazine, "Cosmopolitan Toronto at Lunch," or some such.

I stood on the sidewalk snapping pictures of the general scene, including several of her full face, but she didn't blink an eye. She didn't stand still, either, but I assumed that the camera I had been given could catch her as she moved. I polished my cover story as I clicked away, but she took no notice of me, so I never needed it. A waitress who is late setting up is not to be distracted by a photographer looking for atmosphere to illustrate yet another writer's latest piece on the city's trendy eating spots.

My boss would never stake me a Le Clochard lunch so I walked round the corner to the 401 Building and picked up a sandwich from its café, one of the old garment district's best kept secrets, serving the best and cheapest good, simple food in the area. After graduate school I worked nearby for a while as a shipping clerk in a clothing factory before I got my fingernails on the academic ladder. In that period I ate alternately at the 401 Building or at a tiny and modest French bistro round the corner on Spadina, where the food—mainly things like croque-monsieurs and soup—is the best of its kind in the city, at prices a shipping clerk can afford.

chapter sixteen

That afternoon I had only one class, a poetry group for which a student was scheduled to explicate one of Shakespeare's sonnets, "Let me not to the marriage of true minds". I teach six weeks of poetry in first year, like this: Every day two students are scheduled to explicate a poem. Student A recites the poem, then tells the class how to "read" it, assisted by Student B. Near the end of the hour, it is Student B's turn to read the newly understood poem, sort of "once more, with feeling." As well, the two students each have to submit two five hundred word essays on the poem, one before the hour and one to be handed in later. It is, without doubt, my most successful bit of teaching. On the exam the students must have memorized all eighteen poems so as to identify and state the significance of the fragments I lay out. It's as near as I can get to rote learning. When the students graduate, they know eighteen poems and are grateful to me for life.

Occasionally a student gets in a funk and doesn't appear, then I give the other student an easy time, myself playing B to his A, and I reassign the delinquent with a later place in the schedule. The scheme works very well unless, as today, both students fail to show.

But I have learned to roll with that one, too, and I took out an exercise I had in reserve for just such an occasion, and taught them one or two of "The Ten Uses of the Comma". (In first year we are supposed to devote some classes to grammar and punctuation, and I hold the "Ten Uses of the Comma" in readiness for emergencies). A couple of the exercises are tricky enough so that even students who have been well taught in high school don't get them all right and are intrigued to hear of their mistakes. Usually, I find a little grammar and punctuation goes down very easily. An hour of it, anyway.

When I returned to the office I found a call from Carole waiting for me: Did I remember that we were going to her sister's for dinner? Of course I didn't remember—dining at Carole's sister's was one of the things I took care not to remember. Carole's sister, Arlette, is a psychiatrist, as is her husband, Berky, and though, as I've heard, the demise of Freud ought to have made her cautious, she still trades in insights to the discomfort of her friends and relations; me, anyway. Tonight, though, she might be useful.

I read the message, and noticed only then that there was what I would call an "atmosphere" in the office. Something had taken place, or something would have, something between Ginger and Masaka, something that my arrival had interrupted or prevented from happening. The door was not locked and Masaka's helmet of hair had a still unruffled quietness, but there was an atmosphere, all right; I had interrupted something, and what else could it be but Ginger propositioning her? I am paranoid enough to think that under other circumstances they had been talking about me, but this time I was sure more was going on. For once, it seemed possible that Arlette and Berky might be helpful.

Berky said, "But they *did* send her to university. She has a Ph.D, does she not?"

I had been filling them in on my guess that Masaka, though thirty years old, and a third generation Canadian who had spent five years in graduate school, nevertheless had been protected from the world by her upbringing at the hands of her essentially "old country" parents.

"She will have when she completes her thesis," I agreed.

"One of *those*, is she?" Arlette smiled, then remembered that her compassionate snobbery should include me, also one of those. "What is her topic?" she continued, embarrassed, but not much.

"Jane Austen. I don't know what aspect."

"Really? No time to ask?" She grinned, looking at Carole, who didn't respond.

"What's up," I asked. "What's funny?"

Arlette said, "It's just that you seem to know a lot about her. How long has she been there?"

"I've been trying to make her feel at home."

"What does she look like?"

I was on guard now; they were obviously in a piss-taking mood. "Japanese," I said.

"A huge belly, short, squat, and a giant arse divided by a sash?" Berky asked.

"That's enough. She's small—average for a Japanese, I would think—with black hair, of course, a round face, and what Jane Austen would call a good figure."

"A dish?"

I looked at Berky carefully, but he seemed genuinely interested in his question.

"A Japanese dish: porcelain, fragile, with pretty markings."

"I see. Now tell us about Ginger."

"Before we leave Masaka, you understand my point? I don't think that, in spite of being third-generation, she is entirely Westernized, being carefully brought up, and all."

"Went to college in a closed carriage, did she? Wore a veil? Or just carried one of those big fans they have?"

I decided these two had had enough fun and changed the subject.

"About Ginger," I said. "He's of the earth, earthy, a swordsman from Scunthorpe." I nearly used his joke about himself, but Carole doesn't like jokes built around four-letter words. The actual words as they place themselves naturally in the flow of agitated speech she can accept, even relish, but not their exploitation for comic effect. In other words, when Carole says "fuck", which she has done maybe three times in our relationship, it still sounds the way it would in a Governor General's drawing-room fifty years ago, with an edge which has become blunted in our time. It isn't social decorum that inhibits her, but a fondness for the language. She's taken a vow, for instance, never to use the word "wonderful" unless there's a star in the east.

Berky said, "Coarse fellow, is he? Putting the make on her, too, perhaps?"

"It looks like it, and I don't know if she can handle him," I said.

"Why not? He wouldn't be the first to try, surely."

"I think there may be a cultural problem. Here we have a beautiful, slightly cloistered oriental woman encountering a son of the soil from a male culture trained to jump on anything that moves."

"You think he might try to up-end her between lectures?"

"He's not an animal."

"What, then?"

"I'm concerned they will misread each others' signals. Signals that are instantly recognizable in Scunthorpe, or in Winnipeg, for that matter, she may not be familiar with.

She may misunderstand and respond politely, and then there might be a problem."

Berky said, "Let me get this straight. You posit a situation in which Ginger will act like a nineteenth-century sailor going ashore in Papua, thinking the first bare tits he sees are signalling to him. That's not a good example. Try this ..."

"Never mind, I get the point, and so do you. Yes, I think there's a possibility of cultural misunderstanding."

Arlette said, "Has this Masaka person sent any signals your way? As far as your culture would let you recognize them, I mean."I heard what she was really saying, of course, but I was too curious about the question myself to start shouting at her immediately. The fact is that if Masaka were from my culture I would have found her very much the ice maiden, scrupulously careful in every way to avoid misunderstanding, or, perhaps, in Ginger's case, understanding. "No," I said.

"No little kisses on the brow when you've done a bit of copying for her? No tiny frozen hand on yours to show you how cold it is outside?"

"That's another opera."

Arlette said, "It may be she's so enraptured with you that she's afraid to come too close in case she finds she can't control herself."

I looked around at the trio: two grinning, Carole looking curious. "What am I missing?" I asked

"I'll tell you what we're hearing, shall I?" Berky said. "We're hearing that you're smitten with your new Japanese colleague and projecting your desire onto Ginger. Not making Ginger the object of your desire, of course— no sign of that, is there?—but using him to articulate the effect that Yum-Yum is having on you."

"That's racist," I snapped. "Don't call her that."

"You don't find her tasty?" Berky said. "Tell us, do you think of her outside the office? Do you spend more time than you used to *in* the office? Of course you would have to keep Ginger neutralized. Do you know where she lives? Or whom she lives with? Does she talk Japanese on the telephone, or talk fondly in any language? Have you ever followed her? Bought any green tea yet? Do you dare to eat a peach?"

"Oh, fuck off," I said.

Goddamn psychiatrists. They all think their training equips them with infallible lie detectors, like Hemingway's built-in bullshit detector.

"We'll see," Arlette said. "You've asked them to dinner, haven't you? Can we come?"

"No fear," I said. "Not you two."

Carole said to Arlette, "Let me get a look at them first. Then I'll let you have a look."

"When?"

"Soon."

They were being ridiculous, of course, but time would reveal that. When Carole met her she would see how wrong she was.

In the meantime there were matters in another part of the forest to be attended to. Ever since I had seen Tyler's mistress setting out the tables at Le Clochard, I had been nagged by a sense that I ought to know her from somewhere, so I offered to treat Carole if she would join me for dinner. Since we normally shared expenses, this would be a bit of an occasion.

chapter seventeen

It was raining when we arrived. I found a parking spot round the corner and we were able to scuttle back to the restaurant without getting soaked. The rain worked for me because it eliminated the use of the patio and made it easier to look around inside as I made a business of taking off my coat and wiping my face with a serviette.

She was against the wall right at the end so I ignored the attempt by the host to sit me in the window to make the restaurant look fuller, and took Carole to the back as if to my favourite table. I got it right; she smiled as we approached and started to pour ice water. I got us seated then went to look for the washroom. On my way back I stopped to speak to "Le Clochard" himself who was seated at a little table by the door, adding up the reservations.

"Could you tell our waitress there might be a third person joining us?" I asked him. "I'm half expecting a colleague to show."

"Sure," he said. "But that's okay. Tell her yourself." He went back to counting the take.

"Okay," I said, in turn. "What's her name?"

"Who?"

"Our waitress."

"Which one is she?"

"The one at our table"

"Where are you sitting?"

"Down *there*." Christ. An attempt at a small ruse had created a major "Who's-on-first?" routine. Two waiters and a busboy were listening, intrigued. Now one of the waiters approached. "Whom do you want?" he asked. He was just playing a role, behaving like a snotty Parisian waiter.

"Not 'whom'," I said, and waited, noting with satisfaction the look of uncertainty cross his face. Had he got the pronoun wrong? "What. The name of our waitress."

"Why?" He scrambled to retrieve the snotty look.

"So I can speak to her politely. Okay?"

He shrugged. "Which one is she?"

Eventually I established that her name was Simone, which I saw as soon as I sat down on the label above her left breast. The thing now was to eat as unobtrusively as possible to dampen the now widespread interest in my curiosity about her name. We both had steak frites, a green salad, and a glass of the house red, no dessert, and coffee. You can't eat less conspicuously than that in Toronto.

I had what I needed: a given name, an address, and a car registration. My ex-policeman boss had solid contacts with his former world and by ten o'clock the next morning I had established through the Motor Licence Bureau and confirmed by a city guide that she was Simone Guerriere. I had got several pictures of her, but I still could not put my finger on why she was familiar.

I had a class at ten on Marvell's "To His Coy Mistress", an old war horse I can teach in my sleep, and sometimes have; all you have to do is watch out for the students who may have come across it in high school, and make them tell the class what they already know before you try to say something they don't. Then a little lecture on the importance of the caesura in the heroic couplet generally does the trick of filling out the hour.

After that I drove back downtown to park opposite Tyler's bookshop. My next class was at three, which, even with travelling time and lunch, gave me a couple of hours to spare. I didn't know what I expected to learn by watching Tyler's doorway, but I felt fairly sure that someone familiar would pass through it eventually, someone who would lead me to Mlle. Guerriere.

Half an hour later she appeared; not Simone but my employer, Madame Tyler, the wife, and I saw what had been nagging at me, something any woman would have seen immediately. (And most men, I guess, but for a private detective, I have a lot of trouble registering and remembering faces and attaching names. Recently I asked Carole where we had seen some actress named Julia Roberts before.) Now, though, I had no trouble. Dye Mrs. Tyler's hair blonde, cut it level around the bottoms of her ears, get rid of ten pounds from her chest and slap on a bit of lipstick and there would be the essential Simone Guerriere. These two were probably sisters.

The situation wanted thinking about. My assignment was to confirm that Tyler was having it off on Tuesdays and Thursday nights with one or more women, to put together a report with pictures and present it to Mrs. Tyler so that she, presumably, could make Tyler's life hell before she divorced him. It now looked as if we should move cautiously.

My boss runs the agency from a couple of rooms on the upper floor of a two-story building on the Danforth, and I detoured on my way back to the college to have a chat with him. I laid out the situation for him.

"What are our orders?" he asked. "Remind me."

I spelled them out.

He said, "You think we should tell her it's her sister her old man is bonking?"

"I don't know. That's why I called in before I wrote up my report."

"You don't *know* it's her sister, do you?"

"It could be a cousin, I suppose. No, I don't know, but I'd bet this week's wages on it."

"But you do know her name is Simone Guerriere, right?"

"That I'm sure of."

"Fine. You've done your job. Make out the report. You sure, now?"

"I'm sure they are related."

"Write it up, then, but stick to what you know. I mean you know they look alike, you don't know they're related. And don't forget the picture. I'll give her a call, see if I can get her to say something about the likeness."

By the time I was back in the office, Jack had called. "She wasn't even surprised," he said. "She *acted* surprised—you know, sharp intake of breath, repeating the name, that kind of thing—but it sounded phoney as hell to me. She's up to something more than having her old man watched on his night out."

"So what do we do?"

"Carry on."

"She wants me to stay with it?"

"That's the ticket."

"What's going on, Jack?"

"We'll find out, eventually. In the meantime, I don't have a lot else for you to do. But keep your back to the wall."

"What do you mean?"

"I don't know, Joe. Keep away from him in dark alleys? Yeah, that's what I mean. Keep your distance, and keep your eyes open."

Jack is a romantic. His favourite book is *The Maltese Falcon*. He enjoys the idea of being threatened.

Now I was late for my class. Luckily, today's lecture on Lawrence would practically teach itself, which was just as well because I had only half a mind to spare for the class. I was preoccupied, fascinated, by the phenomenon of the two sisters.

chapter eighteen

Sherbourne Street is only lightly visited by the people I know. At its northern end it crosses Bloor and ends up in Rosedale where Toronto's establishment took root when the great-grandchildren of the original meat-packers and dry goods merchants left their downtown mansions and moved north to escape the new immigrants. Those same descendants now use Sherbourne as a quick route down to the financial district; their ancestral homes have long since been converted into curry houses and steak pits. But now, like most of old Toronto, the street seems to be undergoing another sea change. Boarded-up windows and doors announce, not that the area is becoming derelict, but that new plans are being drawn up, development plans are in the works.

The Garrick was undergoing its own renovation. A new front desk was being assembled and the rest of the lobby was scraped back to the brick shell. A sign said the elevator was out of order, and wooden barricades prevented access to the stairs that had obviously been newly carpeted.

I stood around the lobby for a couple of minutes, then a workman pointed to a door in the back wall. I knocked and a voice shouted, "Come in," and I opened the door and found myself in a tiny business office so new it looked as if it belonged in a showroom. A young man sitting in front of a computer screen waved me in and pointed to a chair by his side. When I sat down our knees brushed together.

"What are you selling?" he asked, as he continued to play with the computer.

"Nothing," I said. "I'm looking for some documents."

"Where did you leave them? Nothing's been turned in."

"I didn't lose them. Someone found them. Here. Maybe fifteen years ago."

He turned off the machine and looked me over. "Are we talking about the famous Hemingway Papers?"

When I nodded, he said. "If you do find them, they belong to me. They were stolen from my father."

I was intrigued. There was an excitement coming off him that had nothing to do with me, but seemed a part of the brand new office and the renovations outside. And he was dressed casually in very expensive clothes, but with no tie. They weren't the clothes of a desk clerk, and he seemed too young to be the manager. On the other hand he was obviously at home, and enjoying himself.

I decided that flattery might get me somewhere.

"Are you the owner, sir?" I said, thinking I would work down from there.

"Yes, I am," he said with a firmness that indicated that he had been asked this question before and was ready for the next one ("Is your mother home?") Then he took off even more years as he added, "Mum is the actual owner, but it amounts to the same thing."

The rapid shift from man to boy, from assistant manager to rich young owner, gave me the feeling I was dealing with a shape-shifter, a happy one.

"So," he said, trying now for briskness. "The Hemingway Papers. They've turned up?"

"I haven't found them," I said. "I was just interested to find out more about them. I heard that they were found here, and then later stolen from a bookseller who was holding them to assess their value. May I ask ...?" I put out my hand.

He looked at it doubtfully, perhaps trying to decide if owners shook hands with people like me. Then he took it. "Gresham," he said. "Larry Gresham. And you?"

"I'm a professor at Hambleton College, interested in Hemingway."

Calling yourself "Professor" is not quite as good as Leacock's calling himself "Doctor" but it still gets you some respect, especially from the young, and professors are among the few people who are still called 'sir' by car salesmen.

"That right?" the hotel proprietor asked. "Do you teach 'The Three Day Blow'?"

The question coming out of mid-air, knocked me off balance. "No," I said. "Well, yes. Sometimes. It depends. Why do you ask?"

"I went to Ryerson," he said. "My dad wanted me to take 'Hotel Management'. We did 'The Three Day Blow' in first year English. The teacher said it was the greatest short story ever written."

This irritated me to the point of forgetting what I was there for. "I could name a few contenders for that prize," I said.

"He said that one was the best." He looked at me brightly.

Get out of this now, I told myself. I nodded just to acknowledge what he was saying, but not to agree with it. "Did you ever see the papers?" I asked.

"What? Oh, sure, I remember them. I was with my dad when he delivered them to Mr. Curry. I was just a kid, but I remember."

"Were you there when your dad threatened Mr. Curry?"

"Who told you that one?"

"All the book dealers I spoke to. Everybody."

He shook his head. "Someone made that up afterwards. Dad didn't threaten anyone. Not in front of me."

"Mind telling me what actually happened?"

"The whole story?"

"If you've got time."

He shifted his shoulders and cleared his throat. I had the impression he was trying to decide which would make him look more mature, telling me what I wanted to know, or saying he was too busy. But it was in his nature to be agreeable, and he began.

"When Dad died, my mom made some changes to this place. She wanted to make the place respectable. When Dad was alive, we had a lot of—er—night trade. You know?"

"I can guess."

"So she set about renovating this place. Got rid of the night trade and the few residents we had, and started redecorating right away. So what do you know, in one of the rooms behind a mirror screwed to the wall there was this big envelope, yea thick." He held his fingers about half an inch apart.

"Do you remember what was inside? Did you see it?"

"Certainly I saw inside, and certainly I remember: I was eleven at the time. A lot of typing, with a lot of crossings-out. Stories. They were probably his first ones, this book dealer said. He recommended Dad let him have them to get them valued."

"James Curry?"

"Huh? Oh, right. The same. So we did. So Dad left them with him."

"Just like that?"

"Dad got a receipt, of course. I've still got it. I don't know where I've put it, but I've got it."

"But your dad did leave them?"

"He did." He looked at me, waiting.

"Then what?"

"Then Mr. Curry was robbed. He kept the papers in a kind of cupboard."

"Locked up?"

"Yeah. In an old wardrobe, like one of those wooden freestanding closets you see in antique shops, with those dinky locks that just keep the door closed; not safe, but private. Someone broke in after hours and busted the door open and took away the papers and a book Dad had found in the same room, behind the radiator."

"A book?"

"You know, a novel, an old one."

"What was it called?"

"I don't know now. Mr. Curry said it might be worth something, and he'd keep it safe until he got it valued, too. So it and the papers disappeared and Dad took after Mr. Curry."

"Did he think he swindled him?"

"At first he did, but then Mr. Curry gave Dad a thousand, and on that he agreed to leave him alone."

"But the papers never turned up."

"Not before Mr. Curry died."

"When was that?"

"Couple of years ago. It was in the paper."

"Let me ask you something," I said, a throat-clearing phrase while I thought of the best way to introduce my next question, one with a slightly delicate subtext. "If those papers turned up now, who would they belong to?"

"That's the question, isn't it? I have the receipt, somewhere."

"And presumably your father signed a receipt for Curry for the thousand dollars?"

"What? Yeah, that's right. Mom's lawyer said he shouldn't have done that. But he says if Mr. Curry claimed he owned them we could claim fraud because Curry was an experienced antique book dealer who knew that those papers and that book were worth a lot more than a thousand dollars."

"But without that, who would own the papers now?"

"My lawyer says maybe the guy who bought Curry's business, including all stock, though we wouldn't agree to that in court, like. How much are those papers worth, do you think? You're a professor."

I had asked Bert Tensor to give me a ball park figure. "Not less than a million dollars," I said.

"Wow! But they haven't turned up, have they? So there's hope for me yet?" He grinned. I gained the impression that he was not taking it very seriously.

"If the papers do turn up, you will probably need to have established a case," I said.

"Beforehand, like?"

"I would think so."

"I'd better find that receipt." He got up and walked to the door, returned, sat down, got up again, sat down again. "Should I get a lawyer?" He grinned. He was still enjoying the story and his role in it.

"Does your lawyer charge much? Maybe you should wait to see if the papers turn up. Your case won't change."

"But you just said ..."

"Tell me," I said, "Did your dad have any contacts who might have any ideas who broke into Curry's store that night?"

"Don't you think Dad tried them? That was before we got renovated and went respectable. Dad said the beer parlour then was the hangout of half the thieves in Toronto. If you had a gold watch to sell you could take it to any of at least three tables to compare prices any night of the week. Mom stopped all that; she proved there was just as much money in a legitimate hotel. She said Toronto was a tourist town, and she set out to cater to them. Put in a nice family restaurant. You know how many people come up from Detroit and Buffalo every weekend? You ever tried to find a room on Caribana weekend? You can't. No way."

"But back then your Dad might have asked these guys in your beer parlour if any of them had been offered any papers lately?"

"He would have kept his ears open, I guess, sure, but I don't remember him saying anything."

"Then or since?"

"I told you, we're legitimate now. I don't hear anything any more." He paused. "Dad did have one idea he told me about. There was a guy named Ted Collier, little rat-faced Irishman who disappeared the day after the break-in, and Dad wondered about him, so he put the word out that he wanted to talk to Collier. He never came, though; Dad never saw him again, no one did."

"Why did he suspect him?"

"Dad said Collier was the type you'd suspect right away, just to look at him, and he was hanging around the lobby when Dad told the desk clerk that if anyone was looking for him he would be at Curry's bookshop. When Dad came back, Cobb, the desk clerk, asked if he wanted to put the parcel back in the hotel safe. Dad told him he'd left it at Curry's. Ted Collier was still in the lobby and he got chatting to the other desk clerk and asked him who Curry was. The clerk told him he was some kind of second-hand book dealer. That was the last we saw of Ted Collier."

"Literally?"

"What? Yeah, the very last. Dad asked everybody he knew, here and across the street, but no one had seen him." He grinned. "Across the street they said it was the longest they'd ever gone without seeing him."

"You've lost me. What's across the street?"

"Back then, across the street was where the police drank. This was before they moved their headquarters over to that building on College Street. My father used to try to get them to come over here for a beer, but they kept to themselves. He stayed on good terms with them, though, always glad to let them know if someone they were interested in was in residence, so to speak."

I was curious. As a part-time investigator I have no status at all with the cops. That's my boss's department, though as his old pals retire he's losing touch a bit. "Didn't you ever get raided?" I asked him.

"Oh, no. We were too useful. My dad was. My dad used to fantasize that one day the cops would recruit everyone in the beer parlour to help them catch some terrible villain, a serial granny-basher maybe, but it never happened. My dad said that as long as they weren't 'wanted' their money was as good as anyone else's."

"You're talking about that old Peter Lorre movie."

"Am I? There you are, then. That's what gave my Dad the idea."

"So when did the policy change?"

"I told you, when my Dad died and Mom and I took over. Now it's my turn."

"You still renovating it?"

"No way. I'm remodelling it. Mom did her thing, and she proved her point. Now I'm going to prove mine. See, I want to take us further up market. You know what a boutique hotel is?"

"I've read about them."

He nodded disappointed, I think, that I wasn't going to encourage him to tell me about them. "We studied them at Ryerson and I used our hotel as a model for conversion for a graduation project. Actually a whole group of us got credit—you know, we formed a kind of consortium. I got a graduate from Interior Design, a guy from Finance—six of us. It was just a project at first, then Mom told me to go ahead, see if I could do it."

"What if it doesn't work?"

He grinned. "Dad left Mom well fixed. She'll be okay."

"Wow!" I said, counted three, then, "And you never saw Ted Collier again."

"Never. Nor did anyone else. Dad even tried to get cute, put out the word that we'd found something valuable of his, he should come pick it up." He grinned. "He never turned up, though."

"What do you think happened to him?"

"For a long time we didn't think anything. We thought he was just staying out of the way, First because he wasn't sure if someone hadn't seen him near Curry's that night, and later just because he was afraid we were on to him. We weren't really; if Collier had turned up the night of the robbery for his usual couple of drafts Dad said he wouldn't have thought anything more of it. But the longer he stayed away the more Dad thought it might mean something.

"So he had another chat with Mr. Curry, and then while Dad combed Toronto, Mr. Curry worked the other end. He sent the word out through the book trade about the missing papers and registered them as stolen and him as owner. That way they could never reach the open market without him hearing about it. As well, all Mr. Curry's contacts in the trade, here and in New York, knew to tell him if Collier turned up with the papers. They had a description—rat-faced, bad skin disease, no teeth, maybe forty but looked a lot older. But we never heard, so we gave up on Ted Collier and Hemingway."

"And you don't have any idea what happened to Collier?"

"The cops said he'd turn up some time, in the lake maybe, but he might not be identifiable so we'd never know."

"Someone might have killed him?"

"Maybe he just lay down and died. Look, Dad said maybe he knew enough to take the papers down to New York and show them around. To the wrong kind of dealer that would be like flashing your wallet around a homeless shelter, downtown, wouldn't it? When I said as much to Mr. Curry once he said no way, book dealers don't go in for that kind of stuff, but Dad always said that if you run a hotel you know there's that kind of stuff in every trade."

"But the papers never came on to the market. Curry would have known, right?"

"He never saw them."

"And Collier?"

"No known relatives, so Dad reported him missing himself. And that was the end of it. Probably still on the Missing Persons file. That never closes on a case, I understand."

"Did Curry have any relatives?"

"A wife, I think."

"So she might have a claim."

"Maybe. Mr. Tyler's the one to ask. She might have stayed in touch with him." He waited to see if I had any more questions.

I stood up, and banged my knees against his. I said, "Mr. Gresham, why is your office so small?"

"This is a boutique hotel. We'll have twice as many rooms in the same space, and I guess I'm setting an example."

As I left, he said, "Can I ask you something? You say you've taught 'The Three Day Blow'?"

"Several times. Why?"

"Who do you think is older, Nick or Bill? We had a big argument in class about it. Our teacher said it was the key to the meaning of the story. You agree?"

"I'm sure he's right. I haven't thought about it much. I'm interested more in the mythical sub-structure."

"Right, the fall, the apple, all that shit. He did that, too, but what really mattered he said, was which one was older."

chapter nineteen

I drove across the city to report to my boss.

"She wants you to stay with it," he said.

"What the hell for? The job's done. We have pictures of the woman her husband is screwing, probably her sister. What more does she want? What is she up to?"

He shrugged. "Maybe once or twice is not enough. As I said, maybe she wants proof of systematic infidelity. I don't know. But don't knock it, Joe. It's cash on the barrelhead."

I told him then of my other current interest in the book trade: *The Case of the Missing Manuscript.*

He listened to the story, then said, "I'll tell you what happened, shall I? The thief got disturbed when he was breaking into the cupboard which, being locked, he assumed contained something valuable. Panicking, but not liking to leave empty-handed, he grabbed a bundle of carefully tied up papers and took off. When he got a chance to look at his loot, he saw that it was just a pile of crap, someone trying to write a book, so he chucked it into a garbage bin on the street."

"So where did Collier go?"

"I'll ask if you like, in case he turned up dead and no one realised they should tell your hotel-keeper. Now, while we're on the subject, you aren't looking for these papers on company time, I hope. You're being paid for surveillance; don't get mixed up in this guy's other antics. He sounds like a chancer to me."

Every now and then, my boss likes to act out his role by talking gruff, but he's an old pussy-cat, really. He enjoys reading about Sam Spade and the boys, but he gets nervous at the idea of doing anything illegal. I think he must have irritated some of his pals on the force.

But I only began asking about the papers out of curiosity, and the quest was beginning to lose its appeal. I was more intrigued by *The Case of the Bookseller's Wife's Sister*, mainly by why the wife wanted me to stay on surveillance now she had all the evidence she needed to get rid of her mate.

I was early to work on Friday morning, not looking for worms exactly, but finding a snake. As I reached the door, Masaka and Ginger sprang apart as she hastily buttoned up her shirt and Ginger crouched behind the desk to hide his tumescence. By the time I opened the door, they were in their normal places, at their desks across the room from each other, but I could tell from the way they both looked up at the same time that I had interrupted them. The point is, even though Masaka, as ever, had not a hair out of place, and Ginger had his cap on, ready to brave the rain-swept streets to get to the Theatre Arts Building (a cap, by the way, a round flat hat, that is so perfect in its pure Newcastle football-stadiumness, that I suspect it of being an affectation, something Ginger bought to come to Canada in, or picked up in Malabar's, the theatrical costumier's on McCaul, to impress any Japanese girls he might meet), there was nevertheless an atmosphere again; again I had interrupted them in some way. Of course it was none of my business, but I didn't like it; Masaka was not equipped to handle the Gingers of this world.

I pretended to have noticed nothing, just reminded them they were both invited for dinner on Saturday. This was Carole's idea; her sister Arlette had been pressing to meet them so Carole gave in and combined the two dinners. I gathered up my poetry text and left.

Two students were outside waiting to make Masaka late for her next class; it was a problem that I had never had, the patient queue of students always waiting at the door. She was a honeypot all right.

My class that morning was examining Wordsworth's "A Slumber Did My Spirit Seal", and the two students who were responsible did a fair job of telling us who and what they thought "Lucy" represented, and then I threw it out to the class and the chattier ones all put in their two cents' worth. Then there was just fifteen minutes for me to ask them when, in the poem, Lucy dies, and tell them, and our time was up. That poem always comes out at exactly fifty minutes.

I went off to meet Richard in the cafeteria to discuss his campaign.

"I wouldn't think you had a chance," I said, when he had brought me my coffee. "Your old colleagues, the part-time staff, can't vote, and they are your only hope. Your new colleagues don't trust you an inch, I'm sure."

"What have you heard? Aren't they split among themselves?"

"The Reds and the Blacks you mean?"

"And the rest, the all-important undecideds. As I see it, the diehard Reds and Blacks are evenly matched. The Reds will vote for Fred Jenkins, all five of them, and the five Blacks will vote for Daniels."

"And the others?" Misanthropes was a good term to characterize the five voters who, while nominally Red or Black, all held grudges against one candidate or the other that went back twenty years; for them, the election was an opportunity to settle accounts.

Richard said, "In the end, the remaining five are two pink, I think, and three grey. If you think of them as a group, if they voted *en bloc* for an outsider, me, I would have a chance."

"What about Riddell?" I asked.

"Forget Riddell. He's just in there to amuse himself. He won't even say what he stands for."

"I know what he stands for. He's a monarchist. That's what he told me on the subway going home."

"And what the hell does that mean?"

"I think it means extremely conservative. He thinks democracy, especially in universities, is self-destructive. He says this college becomes a shambles when traditional university politics—political correctness, affirmative action, the fights against racism, sexism, homophobia— are all invoked and mixed into the question of who to appoint to the chair of the English department. He resents the fact that the ability to write a simple declarative sentence, to punctuate it, to string fifty sentences together into an article that would be acceptable to a real scholarly publication—*The Review of English Studies*, say, not *Oink, the Journal of Animalism*, no longer matters when compared to subscribing to the correct views."

"Put together like that, some of those qualities incline to a pleonasm."

"Not when Riddell is speaking. I'm quoting from memory, probably not doing his style justice. You've got pleonasm wrong there, by the way."

"When did you find this out? I don't remember him making speeches about it."

"You have to put it together from asides, dropped remarks, overheard on the way to a lecture. Usually they sound facetious, but he is absolutely serious."

"What do you know about his position? Presumably if he's to the right of the Conservatives at Queen's Park, then he's all in favour of expanding the Business Division, graduating more of our own M.B.A.'s? That sort of thing? No one here will vote for that, surely?"

"That is clichéd, knee-jerk, leftist sneering. 'Monarchist' doesn't mean 'Libertarian'. Riddell, as a matter of fact, abominates the Business Division." About six years ago, Riddell was the department representative on the Faculty Council. At the second meeting of the year he introduced a motion that Business Studies should be abolished. He said that even a "hands-on" university like this should have a moral core, and he proposed that only programs whose graduates are necessary for the care and welfare of society, or that are entirely useless, should be offered; that we should not offer any programs whose sole purpose was to make the students rich. His particular point was that the purpose of Business Studies is to graduate students who are better at making money than other people, that it is our only entirely selfish program, responding solely to greed. That there is no moral basis to the program is proved, he said, by the proposal to introduce such courses as "Business Ethics", and the like, window-dressing at best, and serving only to give students the vocabulary to handle themselves in debate, or when they are hauled in front of a parliamentary committee investigating aggressive or creative accounting practices, the kind that used to be called crooked.

Richard said, "Would you like some more coffee?"

I began to put my hand in my pocket, Richard having already bought my coffee once, which was unusual in itself in the Hambleton cafeteria, and certainly enough collegiality for one afternoon. Then I remembered. This wasn't a coffee break with a colleague. This was politics. "Yes," I said. "Yes, that would be nice."

When he returned with the coffees, he said, "Would he ban courses in Business everywhere?"

"He wouldn't ban anything, even devil worship. He just wouldn't allow students to study money-lending at the taxpayers' expense. Let those who are inclined, get together and raise the money to study it."

"Now I remember. The motion was defeated, of course, and Riddell resigned and went back to his room. We all thought that the motion was a device he invented to get off council."

"We were wrong. He meant what he said."

"Christ! What else did he tell you between classes? Nothing about the role of the Humanities, I suppose?"

I affected to remember, enjoying myself. "It's coming back to me. Yes, that's it, he thinks that one day someone with his views will be in charge, and will abolish English literature as a subject, at least in its present form. He accepts the position that we don't really teach literature; we can't. We teach criticism, ways of thinking about literature, which he says should be in the hands of people who are trained to think clearly, the Philosophy department."

"So if he were in charge he'd abolish us, and himself, too."

"That's the logical result of his position. But Riddell says he's only human. So long as we know where he stands he will try to keep mum, because he likes his job."

"Which is?"

"Literary appreciation."

"That's all right, is it? A legitimate area of study?"

"Not quite. He thinks it belongs with music appreciation, and art appreciation, and the curriculum should make a place for it as an option to the other 'appreciations', a half-course, say, to be taken any time, like Physical Education used to be."

"One last question: what does he ask them on exams? Now, I mean."

"Mostly to compare and contrast. Compare and contrast one of Shakespeare's sonnets with one of John Donne's, for instance. Or compare Shakespeare's Caesar with Shaw's."

"But ..."

"Go talk to Riddell. He'll tie you up in knots and make you feel like a charlatan."

"I would have time, though, to point out that the whole compare-and-contrast approach to literature was discredited seventy years ago."

"Not as far as Riddell is concerned. He says it's the only way to find out if the students know the text, and knowing the text is all that matters. We make them know the text, and the text does the rest. I think he's got a point."

"You think so? All we have to do is provide him with a forum. As soon as the department hears what he has to say, he'll be finished."

"Possibly."

chapter twenty

The thousand dollars that Curry had paid Gresham, the hotel-keeper, for mislaying his manuscript, was bugging me. It occurred to me that Mrs. Curry, the widow, might be able to help me understand exactly what all that was about. Tensor, my colleague, said she was still alive and living in Toronto; he had been in touch with her as recently as last year. She lived on Lawton Boulevard, north of St. Clair, and Tensor called her for me while I was in his office and arranged for me to see her on my way home that afternoon.

I had one more class, an introduction to *Henry IV, Part One*, an odd choice of play considering it is the only Shakespeare that most of them will get at college, but then most of them have already done the big bow-wow plays in high school and none of us is prepared to teach *Cymbeline* or *Pericles* in first year. *Henry IV, Part One* has turned out to be very popular, which means it has turned out to be very teachable, even by the doubters.

This business of trying to give the students a fresh start after their eight or ten years of English in school is always a problem. It was once suggested that we ask the high schools to steer clear of certain works or areas so as to leave them to us; the high schools quite rightly told us to

get stuffed. I say "quite rightly", because of all jobs, surely the teaching of English in high schools is the hardest.
High school English teachers are entitled to first pick of
everything. The only thing I would ask is that they give us
a year's notice when they want to change the curriculum.

Once upon a time when the department had responded
to a demand from the Writers' Guild that we make
Canadian literature compulsory in first year, I had a student
in Theatre Arts come up to me at the end of the first hour
and say she wanted to switch out of my class. Nothing
against me, she said, but she had no intention of studying
the same novel for the third year in a row, or any of the
other novels on the course, all of which had been rammed
repeatedly down her throat since grade ten (these are her
words) and she was sick of it. Why couldn't she study
Shakespeare, or Milton, or some of these other people she
had heard of?

Rules are rules, of course, but she sounded as if she
might turn ugly, so we made an exception and found a
place for her in "Eighteenth Century and Romantic
Literature", a course offered to third-year Journalists, and
she seemed quite happy with that. But I've digressed again.

When I asked them, it turned out that nobody had read the
play. I got caught out, forgetting that you should never ask
them this question unless it is part of some teaching ploy
you have worked out, because there's nowhere to go if they
all say no. I considered stalking out in a huff but decided
to save that for the next emergency, and chose one of the
livelier students to read the king's opening speech, telling
us what he is saying, line by line, and then we launched
into a brief discussion of the historical context and finally
the "What-kind-of-man-is-he-so-far-as-you-can-tell?"
question which took us until the bell. It wasn't bad for a
Friday, but I made a note that I would need a lively open-

ing for the next class. I warned them to get it read over the weekend, and set off to buy Saturday's dinner.

Lawton Boulevard forks to the left off Yonge Street just north of St Clair Avenue, but to get into it by car, Mrs. Curry explained on the telephone, you have to go left at Heath Street, then right, then right, then left, all before 4 p.m., when it becomes illegal to enter Heath Street from the south.

"We used to be able to turn left into Lawton off Yonge Street," she said, when I met her. "But they put up a 'No Left Turn' sign to protect the neighbourhood some ten years ago, and now it's best to come home along Avenue Road and go downtown via Yonge."

She sat upright in a hard chair, an erect little body in her early seventies, with grey hair cut about an inch long, a sort of sweater dress, dark blue, that came almost to her ankles, and a necklace of big black beads. Her accent was English, Cheltenham Ladies College, I would think, cut glass, quiet and clear. She was being very agreeable. We had tea and some tasty cookies that I complimented her on, thinking she might just have made them herself. She said, "Ikea. I buy my lingonberries there, too. Very good with vealburgers."

"Really?" I said. "Next time I serve vealburgers I'll go out to Ikea first."

She might have been offended, but she smiled. "Don't make fun of me," she said.

I liked her a lot. There was that about her smile, a look of being permanently amused by the world, including me, that might have put some backs up, especially with the accent, but I decided she was just inviting my complicity in finding the world risible.

I looked around the room, feeling the need to test my voice before I began asking questions. There were the usual chairs and rugs and pictures and so on, and I couldn't find anything to say about them until I realized what was missing. Books: there were no books.

"Books do furnish a room," I said.

She caught it, of course. "So said Virginia, but she wasn't married to a book dealer. I detest books as things, and after James died I got rid of them all and I've never given house-room to a book again, once I've read it. I read, of course. Old favourites. I can't be bothered to sort out all the voices that tricky moderns use. I like a book to start off with the narrator telling me where and when he or she was born. I go to the library every week. I like saucy novels, too; I can't wait for the next Carl Hiassen—but I always give them away when I've finished. The thing is, antiquarian booksellers are obsessed. I mean, if you marry a mailman or an airline pilot, they don't talk about postage or ice on the wings all the time, do they? But book dealers do. Books, books, books. I refused to have them to dinner. Book dealers, I mean. But I did love James. What can I do for you, Mr. Barley?"

There was a pause of two or three seconds while I realized that she had finished on an interrogative note. I explained my mission.

She rose from the chair without difficulty. "There will be a copy of the receipt," she said. "Pour yourself another cup of tea. The lavatory is through that door," she added, using the naked-sounding English term, a word that delivers a tiny shock to North American ears, familiar only with the euphemisms.

I didn't need the lavatory so I had time for three Ikea oat crisps before she returned waving a half-sheet of paper. "This explains it," she said. She lowered herself on to her chair, still holding the paper. She looked it over before handing it to me. "I thought your account sounded odd. What you said about James paying Gresham off, I mean. As far as I remember from the days when I used to listen to James when he talked about books, no reputable dealer would have paid out money like that. He would never have pretended to own such a valuable property, no, he would have agreed to represent it only, to sell it on to a collector, or one of the big American dealers, but he wouldn't have given Gresham some kind of partial payment. It would have caused a muddle, as it seems to have done.

"James was simply protecting his right to represent it, to agent it, horrible verb. You see, he would have put in a fair amount of work on those papers, and he would not want Mr. Gresham to decide to take them to another dealer after all. No, the thousand was really given to create a contract."

I wasn't convinced. "Mrs. Curry, I know your husband's reputation was that of a dealer of integrity ..."

She broke in. "Shall I tell you how he used to categorize his colleagues?" Her voice was full of glee at what she was going to say. "First, he said, there are the Sleazes. Those were the dealers who were as bad as the public. No, don't draw back. Think of the public with a capital P, the two or three per cent of the customers who set out to swindle the dealers. When you hear of a book dealer referring to the public, be sure to know if he has just had a book stolen by someone with a capital P.

"Then there is the second category, the Fools, the ones who cheat you out of ignorance. I was never very clear about this category, but it, too had a capital, and James was pleased to have invented it. Then there are the Corner Cutters, basically good chaps, even the women, who feel it is their duty to cheat the rich but not the hard up. James thought that Corner Cutters were the thin end of the wedge. Finally there were James and his trusted friends, truly honest men all. Dealers are dealers, of course, and they have a duty to make a profit, but, well, a reputable dealer doesn't pretend a thing isn't valuable if it is." She ended, "Now look at the receipt in your hand."

I read it carefully. I said, "It's not clear to me that this isn't a receipt to satisfy Gresham, to buy him off when the papers disappeared."

She twinkled. "If you were a proper detective, you would see it immediately, but now I'm holding on to it as a surprise."

"So be it," I said. I finished my tea and stood up. "I still think you are the rightful owner."

"That's very sweet of you," she replied.

I got nothing more out of her.

I left her and drove along Gormley to Oriole Parkway, from where I had to pick my way across town to Spadina, then I turned south to Elizabeth Street and the old Jewish market. The Old Jewish Market ought now to be capitalized, because it is a place name, not a description. It's a Portuguese market now, becoming West Indian, with a couple of New Age restaurants selling falafel and such, and the old synagogues have all turned into experimental theatres, so it's a mish-mash, but one or two of the original shops have survived, including the European Meat Market.

This was one of those times when I was up for cooking one of my three specialties, baked ham, the oldest item in my cuisine. Once, when I was even poorer than I am now, before I met Carole, the European Meat Market was recommended to me as a place to buy the cheapest pot roast south of Highway 401—I was feeding a bunch of graduate students that night, and a big pot of stewed meat and onions looked feasible—but the store owner persuaded me to buy a ham, explaining to me how to cook it and serve it. I was nervous, because I was still living on wieners and beans, but he guaranteed the result and I bought one of his smoked picnics for about six bucks and took it home and cooked it. He was right.

The price of ham had gone up a bit; this time I paid ten dollars. I took it home and boiled the smoke out of it for about three hours, and set it out to cool. The next morning, while Carole was getting on with Peter Ackroyd's *Biography of London*, whose eight hundred and some pages were hers for the weekend, I stripped off the skin, cut away most of the fat, and mixed up my secret basting sauce (Rombauer, p. 637, in Carole's edition). All I had to do then, on Saturday morning, was drive down to the other market, the St. Lawrence Market, pick up a strudel from the Mennonite family stall in the north market across from Harlan Clark, the egg man, and some extra hot mustard in the south market from Tom, behind the counter at Anton Kozlick's (I get many compliments on my mustard), a lot of potatoes and some broccoli. We already had the grated cheese to sprinkle on the broccoli, because we use it on spaghetti.

In the afternoon I peeled enough potatoes for six with an extra one for Ginger, and sliced them up for my (Julia Child's) special scalloped potatoes. Half an hour before the guests arrived, I would put the ham (studded with cloves and basted) in the oven, drain the potatoes and put them in a big baking dish with salt, pepper, garlic, and milk, and put the strudel out ready to shove into the hot-but-cooling oven once the main course was on the table. And that's it.

Carole said, "Anything I can do?" although she didn't look up when she said it, but that's all right. I liked the offer but didn't need the help, because I cook this three times a year, at Easter, Thanksgiving, and on Boxing Day, warning Jewish friends what they are in for. As the man from the meat market promised, it always works.

I have developed one other major dish, a lamb stew, for people who have had the ham twice, and for casual occasions I have learned to trust the recipe for chili in *The Silver Palate* cookbook.

Carole also can assemble three dishes by heart, so it takes a long time before new friends get the same thing twice.

chapter twenty-one

An old professor in graduate school told me that once upon a time men always wore shirts and ties when invited to friends' homes for dinner. Academics usually wore tweed jackets, too, as a mark of the profession, the way clerics wore dog collars, then. The women wore dresses and shoes with heels. That was just before the Beatles, as the poet said. Nowadays anyone who turns up in a tie is between seventy-five and eighty, and cites Danielle Darrieux as his favourite actress.

The sixties muddied the concept of appropriate costume, as the age confused everything else, this old professor said (he taught French, hence the choice of favourite actress), with the result that you can't see any more by his outfit if he is a cowboy. He might be being whimsical, or even ironical. I was reminded of that old professor's comment when the first guests arrived.

Ginger came early with Masaka whom he had collected en route—neither one has a car, so they walked over together. Ginger lives on Macpherson, within reach of all that *Toronto Life* has to offer, although slightly farther north than the late night street scene. On Sundays, Ginger walks in his orange boots, exploring the city, mapping it mentally, district by district, and he knew the way from his house to our apartment without directions or maps.

Masaka also likes to walk in the city. She has a room in the Annex, on Dupont Street, so it was easy for them to meet on the corner of Dupont and Spadina. It's only a few more blocks to our place and you might wonder, as I did, why Ginger didn't call for her, wonder if it isn't one more convention that has disappeared.

Ginger wore a dark blue Harris tweed jacket, grey flannel slacks, highly polished black loafers, a blue-checked button-down chambray shirt, and a blue and white striped tie. Apart from the day of his job interview, when he wore a suit, which he told me later he had rented, I could not remember ever seeing him before without his orange construction boots, his moleskin trousers, and his knobbly sweater.

"My God," I said, then checked myself, for which I was later very proud. I was about to say something crass like, "You didn't have to get dressed up for us," forgetting how that remark, intended to put the visitor at ease, in fact makes him feel totally gauche, a bumpkin, someone who "dresses up" in his "Sunday-go-to-meeting clothes" when he is an invited guest.

As I say, I caught myself in time. What I said was, "My God ... there really is a Scunthorpe tie," and learned thus how close I had come to disaster, how aware Ginger was that something about him might be odd, even risible, because he didn't smile but responded warily, with a closed face, "It's Leeds University, actually."

I started to introduce him to the others, my mind struggling with the question, still very much there, of why he *had* dressed up. And then I got it. Masaka, of course. It was she he was tarted up for, not us.

I skidded past him now to take her by the hand. She also was looking striking, but happily so, in a grey silk dress, sleek hair, and as far as I could tell, no make-up, just an apricot-coloured complexion and a smile that wrinkled her nose and closed her eyes. I could even revisit my childish belief that her perfume was not in fact perfume, but her.

I tried to guess from her demeanour whether Ginger had tried to have his way with her already, in her room, getting there early, but she was as inscrutable as ever. And then she asked, "Do you approve?" to let me know I was staring a bit hard and overlong at her, and I took them both into the kitchen to meet Carole who was cutting carrots and zucchini into small pieces to be offered along with Ziggy's tangy vegetable dip with the pre-dinner drinks.

And now I noticed that even Carole, who normally wears one of my old shirts and a pair of blue jeans for informal entertaining, had put on a dressy black and white sweater and a skirt I couldn't remember having seen before. What was going on?

The question only intensified with the arrival of Arlette and Berky. Arlette has a nice pair and tonight she was displaying them under a blouse that seemed to need an extra button and offered a visual Alpine pass down to her navel. Below this, she had on black tights and sort of ballet slippers, and I had to resist the urge to snap my fingers in facetious tribute while humming something from *Carmen*. She was clearly self-conscious enough without that.

And then, finally, came Berky, who, like me, normally eats at our apartment dressed in a clean sweatshirt and chinos, but was tonight wearing a brand-new fawn leather jacket that must have cost him a thousand dollars, over a cashmere-looking wheat-coloured sweater with a little collar, brown pants, and Italian-looking shoes made of what appeared to be highly polished light brown paper. The only way to read all this dressing up was to see it as their separate sartorial responses to what they had heard (or, in Ginger's case) already knew about Masaka. Luckily my own dove grey sweatshirt was brand new and I had forsaken my track pants for a pair of chinos, ironed, for once, or I would have started jeering at everybody's duds (Why are you all dressed up?) in self-defence.

I opened the wine that Berky and Ginger had brought. Berky had splashed out for a *grand cru* while Ginger sought to make his mark with one of those giant litre-and-a-half bottles of country red from upstate New York. I poured everyone a drink, put the potatoes in the oven, and filled the broccoli steamer with water.

The chat consisted mostly of hilarious anecdotes we had all heard dozens of times, except Ginger and Masaka, of course, who were the excuse for trotting them out again, and an animated discussion of the best way to walk the ten blocks from Masaka's room to our apartment. Half an hour later we sat down to eat.

I was a little nervous about the food. Although sure that ham and potatoes would suit Ginger, and that Arlette and Berky had known what to expect, I wondered if ham meshed with Masaka's culture—kobe pork?—and I hung over her a bit, ready to scramble some eggs or defrost a piece of haddock, but she did the trick that beauties like her always manage, of vacuuming up her share when you turn your head away and coming back for more. So that was all right.

There was nothing stimulating about the rest of the conversation, over dinner and into the evening, but it never lagged as all of us worked like dogs to enliven the banal: old anecdotes, jokes, preferences, memories of Spain, all trotted out as bright as when they were first coined. I had bought a bottle of port for a lark, but Ginger was the only one not to raise an eyebrow at it, so I didn't bother to open it.

The women finished the good wine, Berky and I drank from Ginger's flagon of Adirondack Red, and Ginger himself found my beer and drank off a bottle with the relief of someone from Scunthorpe who had been served hot saki and only that all night. Berky and I ended the evening with a little Scotch, and I became on edge in anticipation of the last phase.

Walking Masaka to the party had been fair enough but I felt some obligation to discourage Ginger from assuming that the whole evening had been a prelude to bedding her—why else was he dressed up except to get undressed?—and when it turned out to be raining and the offers of rides started to appear, I tried to assign myself to driving Masaka home, with some protest on her part, but Carole said I had had one too many drinks and felt it looked more responsible to the cops to see a woman driving after midnight, so Carole took Ginger home, leaving Masaka to Berky.

And thus, when I came back from waving them all goodbye from the doorstep, Arlette was waiting for me. I sat down across from her as she said, "We've got about twenty minutes."

I knew what she was saying, and I wasn't surprised; to explain why I wasn't, I need a flashback.

chapter twenty-two

I had known Arlette as a quasi-sister-in-law for three years, as long as Carole and I had been together. We fed each other, the four of us, on a monthly basis, our baked ham or butterflied lamb leg or whore's spaghetti or pot roast cooked in beer, alternating with her surprises which chiefly derived from the cuisine of the middle and far east as filtered through the Review section of the Saturday paper. I'm not crazy about shish kebab sprinkled with lavender (her latest), or stir-fried roots of any kind. Such food makes me develop a hankering for the meat loaf sold in the Winnipeg Eaton's of my youth, with mashed potatoes and turnips, followed by apple pie with a bit of cheddar on top, but there's no way I'm going to get them when Arlette is cooking, or to be fair, Carole, either, although Carole doesn't weigh herself after every meal like her sister, so there's hope. Very rarely, we all eat out together at a fish restaurant because both women are nervous about cooking fish. We don't socialize beyond that.

Thus far my relationship to Arlette had been entirely verbal and totally unambiguous. I had never thought of her as other than my common law sister-in-law, and then only in her presence. Away from her I never gave her a thought, and I assumed that I occupied as little space in her thoughts. And then, starting about six weeks ago, I became aware that our conversations were becoming charged with more than politeness. Later, scouring the memories of our most trivial exchanges for clues, I came to what I thought was the beginning, a light chat one night about that confession on television of a former American president who, though he had never practised adultery, confessed to occasionally having "lust in his heart" for other women. (This interview took place within living memory.)

Somehow, it seemed to me, Arlette contrived to create a conversation when she and I were alone in which she invited me to speculate on the former president's remark, to the point where I think I said, still lightly enough (always trying for a quip), that the heart was the place for love, all right, but lust was seated somewhere else. I didn't think much about it, but I believe I meant what I said. I probably winked, too.

And then, within two or three further chats, I found myself being invited to identify the women, or at any rate the kinds of women who stirred me.

Now I became aware that we were having an extended but interrupted single topic conversation and I became wary, and curious. Arlette is a psychoanalyst, and I didn't trust her an inch with my secrets, and I didn't trust myself not to accidently reveal them. But it seemed to me that she might simply be using me as a case study, trying for some general information, so I didn't challenge her, or tell her the truth, of course. I quite understood that if she told me the purpose of her questions, the knowledge would modify my answers and perhaps invalidate them. It's an old game, after all.

But I was more careful henceforth, and then quite abruptly, the topic changed. As the climax to a conversation several weeks before in which I had been talking a little bit about myself—and my teaching, I think—Arlette had said, "I think your students are pretty lucky, Joe, and I know Carole thinks *she* is. I guess you wouldn't want to

upset a world like that, would you." She spoke rhetorical-
ly, but a ghost of a question mark remained, I thought.

We got interrupted soon after that, but not before she
had had a chance to pay me one or two more compliments.

I've had my share of flattery, of course, and it always
works, but there was something extra here, I thought,
more going on than simply a spontaneous cheer for me,
something earnest about her delivery that sent off alarm
bells. I tried to turn the conversation, but she kept it up,
finding several more ways to identify my wonderfulness.
Whatever I did or said next would be crucial to the calm
of my domestic world. I had to have a second or two to
run through the possibilities before I dealt with them, and
then, having decided what Arlette was up to, figure out the
least damaging response. Damaging to her, I mean,
because she had made herself very, very vulnerable; I
guessed that if I didn't use the utmost circumspection she
might do me serious damage to protect her nakedness, perhaps even refusing to socialize in the old way over the
baked ham and Polynesian stir-fries and such. She might, I
feared, construct for Carole a scenario in which her words
could be defended. She might even try to kill me.

While I was organizing my thoughts, there was the
sound of people coming back, and eager to give myself
some breathing room, I said, "Whatever's happening to
you, Arlette, let's keep control of it. Berky's on his way."
You could read the words as completely impersonal,
"whatever" meaning some alien element, a powerful
aphrodisiac perhaps, that someone, probably Ginger, had
slipped into the wine.

Arlette said, "To me?" I didn't see the significance of
her tone of wonder until much later. She turned away and
sat down on the couch, reaching for her wineglass, and
got ready to deliver her news, news which I very much
wanted to cut off. Something said is very hard to unsay,
and I was sure I knew what she wanted to say, and if she

got the chance to say it the world would change. Happily, the others arrived at that point, bringing the outside world with them.

Now, on this night, Arlette was once again resuming the conversation, but I was ready for her. I risked a little hand-patting, to her surprise apparently, which in turn surprised me. I settled myself away from her. I said, "I've been thinking. I want to tell you something about me."

She said, "I'm listening."

I said, "Does Carole ever hint to you about our love life? Mine and hers, I mean."

"Carole? You crazy? She's the most private person I know. She probably doesn't even hint to *you* about your love life."

I laughed, liking Arlette a bit more. "All right, then, just so you'll know it's not you, I am currently and I hope temporarily suffering an acute loss of libido."

"It's libeedo, not libydo."

"Libeedo, libydo: both are acceptable. In *Webster*, anyway."

"Been reading up, have we?"

I said, "Arlette, I haven't had a fuck for a month or a wank for a year. No, that's the wrong way round. I mean I haven't had a wank for a month or a fuck for a year."

Here is where her training came in. I was trying to shake her, but she heard this kind of thing every day, of course, though not in the same terms. She said, "What's a wank?"

I explained, feeling silly. "It's not a Canadian word," I said. "Actually, the whole sentence is a quote from a letter of an English writer I've been reading at breakfast."

"Is it true?"

"Well, no, not literally, not of me. This writer's about thirty years older than me. I was just using him as an example, trying to kind of epitomize what I think is the low libido state, in case I had the term wrong. This same writer wrote a whole novel about it."

There was the sound of someone in the hall downstairs. Once again I put in a solid quarter of a minute's thought. Arlette was looking at me in wonder. "Let me call you," I said. "I just wanted to explain why my response to the way you feel has nothing to do with you. It's me."

She stared at me, understanding showing on her face, but before she could say anything they were on us. Here I had an inspiration. We were a very agitated-looking pair and some questions would be raised, so, as the door opened, I sprang on her and rumpled her deeply, kissing her teeth, as she, catching the idea that I was now larking about (I have that reputation), kissed me back.

"Happy New Year to you, too," Berky said, as we sprang apart.

"Berky!" I cried, theatrically. "It's no use. In vain have we struggled …"

"That's a quote," Berky said, slightly indignant. "Even I know it."

"Of course, but it expresses exactly how I feel about Arlette. You must yield her up, Berky. She and I …"

"We were just wondering how you were making out with Nanki-Poo," Arlette cut in, helping me out. "We thought we had time for a bit on the side."

Berky laughed indulgently, recognizing horseplay for what it was. "Nanki-Poo wouldn't let me get to first base," he said.

"You tried?" Arlette asked.

"Of course not. I just knew."

And so on.

chapter twenty-three

O n Sunday I woke up feeling thoughtful. Life had
rearranged itself as it is apt to do at the onset of
desire. I wondered what would happen next, sure only that
I hadn't seen or heard the end of Arlette.

I had no idea if her obsession with me would continue,
and what form it would take if it did. Would she hang
around the corner of Dupont and Howland, waiting for
Carole to go out? Would I find her waiting for me at the
college? I remembered one of my tenured colleagues having to deal with the problem of a professor of Philosophy
with whom he had flirted at the annual faculty association
party who spent all her spare time for the next three weeks
in his office when he was there, so that he couldn't get his
marking done. He found her there when he came back
from class, and they had coffee together, and lunch every
day that their schedules allowed it. After three weeks of
complaining bitterly to his male colleagues, who offered
him advice on how to get rid of her, he left his wife and
moved in with the philosopher, just as his female colleagues, who had never believed in the one-sidedness of the
affair, had expected. I had no idea if Arlette would decide
to pursue me; I didn't have much idea of her at all.

The phone rang, Carole picked it up, said "Hi, Arlette," and the sheets on my side of the bed grew damp and cold. I waited while Carole listened to what was obviously an outpouring of Arlette's need for me, wondering what Carole's response would be, beyond offering to call back when she was finished reading the chapter she was on. Carole said, "Well, no, I didn't mind the guy," and "No, not a rough diamond, more of a whatdoyoucallit, a noble savage, no, that's not right, a natural something, anyway. You wouldn't know he was studying English."

I gathered it wasn't me but Ginger they were anatomizing. They moved on to Masaka, and now Carole's replies grew monosyllabic as she tried to choke Arlette off and get back to her book. Carole doesn't like chatting on the phone, or in person, either, for that matter. When I first met her at a party in Cabbagetown, she was in the room with the coats, reading a book. She must have found the subject of Ginger particularly interesting to be worth this much time on the phone. Arlette seems to be all Carole needs by way of society—Arlette and me, a good bookshop, and a video rental store that specializes in classics. Periodically some woman who is wondering whether I am worth bothering with and who prides herself on her social skills will hint at a curiosity about what I see in Carole. I have to deflect this curiosity, because the answer doesn't exist in terms of qualities to be added together to form a desirable mate, but in the simple fact that I can't get enough of her.

Carole listened now for a long time and with far more patience than usual to what I decided was a one-sided discussion of Masaka as the result of Berky's report. That was my guess because earlier in the conversation Carole had said, "Joe says he likes her patellas; pretty, heart-shaped, he says they are," and it sounded as if they had moved on from there. Then Carole said, "He's a good chatter-upper, is Joe. I'm surprised you haven't noticed it before. Well, no, not around here. The week after next, then. What colour wine? Right. 'Bye."

She put down the phone and picked up her book. I said, "Arlette have anything to say, post-mortem-wise?"

Carole looked up and staged a show of looking around and vaguely identifying me for the first time to remind me that I was interrupting her Sunday morning reading. "She said you and she had a nice tête-à-tête. That right?"

Perfect. Arlette had obviously only called in case the balloon had gone up, and this rubbish about a tête-à-tête was designed to integrate with any comment I may have made to Carole already about how Arlette and I had passed the time at the end of the evening, assuming I hadn't told the truth. We were going to hang on, apparently, until we could meet again.

Cheered, relieved, and needing to express it, I said to Carole, "I want you first; then we'll walk down to Mel's for bagels and lox."

"One page," she pleaded.

I nipped across the hall to brush my teeth, passing her on the way back. When she returned, she said, "No foreplay, please. Just bang away. Okay?"

I made a mental note to check on what she had been reading that morning.

After breakfast we crossed Bloor Street and dawdled among the remainder counters of Book City, Carole's ideal store because it has the best sales in town. When you read as greedily as she does, cost is a factor.

I suggested a stroll afterwards, but she had some work she had been postponing, and I was happy to play the footloose bachelor for a couple of hours. I walked down Major Street, hoping to bump into someone I knew; half the people I know live on Major Street, but they were all eating dim sum down on Spadina, I think, and I continued south without a single greeting, to the market, which is nice and crowded on Sunday mornings.

I don't know what I expected to learn by looking at the outside window of the love nest on a Sunday morning when Tyler was presumably elsewhere eating brunch with his wife, and maybe his wife's sister. But the job was on my mind. I don't normally get much opportunity to turn my night job into a detective story, but Tyler and his ménage seemed to offer all the ingredients I needed to think one up. Something was going on—collusion, maybe? Why else would Mrs. Tyler not have reacted, or reacted so little to the discovery that Tyler was diddling her sister? I was sure she wasn't even surprised, that her reaction was faked.

"Back again, eh?" a voice said. The sausage seller had his cart on a wide section of the sidewalk. He was advertising Polish, Italian, and German sausages, and jumbo hot dogs. "What'll it be?" He pointed to his list.

The word "again" triggered some caution in me. In spite of being full of bagels and cream cheese and smoked salmon, all washed down with two cups of coffee, instinct told me to buy a knackwurst and find out what he knew about me. I showed him a two-dollar coin. "Still at the old stand?" I said.

But he just took the toonie and gave me a hot dog, the only thing he offered for the price. "Until the cops move me on," he said.

I adjusted the paper napkin around the hot dog, searching for an opening.

Then he said, "No car today?"

So he did know me from seeing me at work, then, on Tuesday and Thursday nights. "You've noticed," I said, nodding, grinning.

"Having trouble with the wife?"

I had to decide whether to resent his assumption that I was spying on my wife, or use it. In the short term, I decided it could be helpful. "You've got it," I said, adopting a disgusted air.

"I've seen you in your car, watching them," he said, unnecessarily nodding up at the windows of the love nest.

"You ever seen them when I'm not around?"

"Never. I noticed that. Why is that?"

"Those are the nights she says she goes to Yoga."

"Yoga? Kama Sutra more like it."

I was impressed, but it probably takes very little knowledge of English to include the Kama Sutra in your reading, and the sausage vendor was fluent enough.

"You know what you have to do?" he asked.

Now he had me, curious to learn what a sausage seller with old country values would do about an errant wife. Kick her out of the house? Flog her? Chain her up? Give her father his money back? "What?" I asked.

He nodded and winked, first with one eye, then with the other. I've never seen such lasciviousness conveyed with only two eyes. "Every night," he said. "Try it when you get home. That'll stop her."

At another time I might have tried to find something to say that would have dissociated myself from this gargoyle, but this wasn't the time. "Quilp's remedy," I said. "Maybe I'll try it."

"Who was that? Quilp who?" He pointed across the street. "Someone's trying to get you to notice him," he said.

It was Glinka, Tyler's landlord. "Still looking for a room?" he shouted across the traffic. "Come on over. I'll show you something."

The sausage seller said, "That's a clever idea," and turned to serve a customer.

chapter twenty-four

I ran through a gap in the traffic and joined the landlord on the sidewalk. There was a garbage disposal bin a few feet away; I checked that the sausage man wasn't watching before I dumped the hot dog in the bin.

"Why did you buy it if you didn't want it?"

I saw that the truth would keep us there for some time and he would possibly guess what I was really doing. Fortunately, he was almost certainly from a Greek Orthodox world, which gave me my out. I said, "I forgot what day it was. I haven't been to Mass yet."

"You Roman?"

"Old Catholic," I said. "There aren't too many of us in Toronto. Why did you call me over? Do you have a room?"

I thought he might persist and ask me where the church was, but he let it go. "Soon, I think," he said. "The one I showed you, you were interested in."

"He's given notice?"

"He didn't pay his rent this month. Same thing. His deposit runs out in a week. You still looking?"

"I've seen a few other places, but I like yours best. Could I have another look while I'm here?"

My idea was not to look again at the room, but from it, through the window, out on to the street where we were now standing. It had occurred to me that I was being set up in some way, that while I was watching Tyler, he was watching me; at least, keeping tabs on me, in which case I should report to Mrs. Tyler that he had become suspicious and would probably find a new place to meet his lover.

I was trying to think about something that had bothered me from the beginning, that if you want to have a discreet affair you don't do it with the light on behind a see-through blind so that Harbord Street can enjoy the show. I shouldn't have assumed that Tyler was stupid or careless.

"Sure," the landlord said. "It's Sunday, like you say. He never comes on Sunday. Come on up and look at it and then afterwards you can go to Mass."

As we walked the length of the building to get to the side door, I glanced across the street and saw that the sausage vendor was watching us with interest. There was nothing I could do about it, except remember if he accosted me again that to him I was just a gutless cuckold trying to check up on my wife.

The landlord led the way upstairs and along the corridor to Tyler's love nest. "It's okay, even if he comes along," he said. "Not paying the rent is like giving notice so I'm entitled to show people the room. Right?" He unlocked the door and waved me in. "Still, I'll go back to the stairs. If he comes in, I'll make some noises and you can come out. Better not upset him. Don't touch anything, okay?" He walked back to lean against the door to the stairs, listening for newcomers.

There was nothing more to learn from the room. The cot had been neatly made up with a couple of cushions to resemble a couch. The only other furniture was the chair and the table.

I walked over to the window to see what I could and had to step back quickly as I realized that I was in full view of the sausage vendor, luckily just then making a sale. But even from the middle of the room I could survey all the parking spaces I used regularly, and again I had that tremor of uncertainty, the feeling that I was being observed. If Tyler had the slightest tremor of his own, he was bound to get me in his sights, and surely that was why he was abandoning his love nest. It would only be fair of me to let Mrs. Tyler know this, and to put another watcher on the job, because next time, Tyler would be very careful to make sure I wasn't out there watching him.

"Seen enough?" Glinka said. He was standing in the doorway, his keys in his hand.

"I like it," I said. "Would you let me know when it's vacant?"

"I got your number." He turned to lead me down the hall. I made to follow him when I noticed as I stepped around the wastebasket a small familiar-looking paper envelope, about three inches square with a drawing of a pirate's face and the words "Ho-ho-ho" printed on it. I grabbed it and stowed it away in a pocket. Surely Mrs. Tyler would not need more evidence than this.

Glinka opened the door at the bottom of the stairs and led me outside. He nodded to the other side of the street, "Your pal is waving to you," he said.

It was the sausage vendor again. It occurred to me that the vendor himself was in a position to be a first-class snoop, and I crossed over to see if he had anything special to say that could interest me.

"I seen you talking to Glinka," he said. "I figured you out. You're asking Glinka about the room next door."

"Why would I do that?"

"I seen it in the movies. Glinka's place is made of chipboard. You put a glass to the wall and stick your ear in it, you can hear all that they're saying. And doing." He winked three quick winks with the same eye, then stuck an inch of tongue out of one corner of his mouth, and crossed his eyes. He looked like something carved on the underside of the seat in a mediaeval cathedral to remind worshippers of their lower natures. I moved to dissociate myself from his earthy fancies. "That how you get your jollies?" I asked. "Thinking up stuff like that?"

It was a mistake. He could find nothing to say, but his attitude made it clear that I was making an enemy, and I remember the saying that you should choose your enemies carefully. I had a feeling I had been careless.

"Just kidding," I said. "You think that glass trick works?"

He remained wary. "So they tell me."

I said, "I'll let you know," and I think it was just enough.

He said, "You do that."

chapter twenty-five

I walked along to Spadina and caught a streetcar, full of Chinese shoppers, up to Bloor, and walked the rest of the way home. I waved through the glass windows of three cafés at people I knew, recognized without claiming the acquaintance of four others; which is what I like about Toronto. Montreal is a more sophisticated city, but Toronto is Canada's largest village. I wound up back at Book City where I bought a Sunday *Star*, and crossed over to Howland and home.

I've given up newspapers on a daily basis. It wasn't easy, because I'm addicted to print, especially in the morning, but I realized lately that I am using all my best morning energy trying to keep track of on-going news stories written and read only because the newspaper is printed every day. First I cancelled my subscription and for a few weeks bought a paper as soon as I got out of the apartment. Then I worked at buying it later and later in the day (it's a bit like giving up smoking) and found that the later I bought it, the less interesting it was. I had already seen the headlines in newspaper boxes maybe twenty or thirty times by then, and however dramatic they seemed in the morning, the world was always there eight hours later. So the day came when I didn't buy one at all and it didn't make any difference to my social or intellectual life, and two weeks later I had almost no cut-down trees on my conscience when I put out the paper garbage. To be honest, the trees were never a major concern, but it was a pleasant bonus.

What I do in the mornings now, to satisfy my need for print and to avoid making Carole talk to me, is work my way through some very large books, a chapter a day. The Russians, Dostoyevsky and Tolstoy, were an obvious beginning, big novels I'd read once but too quickly, then George Eliot and Fielding, Thackeray and Theodor Dreiser, and then I came to Dickens, and I'm still on *Nicholas Nickleby* (I think I'm reading them in the reverse order of composition, but it doesn't matter; no one is going to examine me, and who can face *Barnaby Rudge* first thing in the morning?) Every morning for the last week I've woken up hoping today is the day when Nicholas and Smike join the Infant Phenomenon and the rest of them and head for Portsmouth. You can't do that with the *National Post*.

On the weekend, though, I buy the Saturday *Globe* because it's full of agreeable gossip, about books and movies and such—comic pages for adults, really, a paper for a day off—and on Sundays I buy the *Star* to find out from its columnists what to think about the week's events, and from its book pages what not to read.

"Arlette called."

Carole scrunched up the slip of paper and returned to staring out the window with the book in her lap. The writing of messages on paper was something that I had insisted on in the early days of our relationship when I realized that Carole kept her mental place in the book she was reading even as she answered the phone. The message itself, if it was for me, often never got through. She would remember on good days that the phone had rung, that the call had been for me, and on very good days who had called, but almost never beyond that.

"What did she want?"

Carole tried to focus. "Who?"

"The woman who called. You know. Your sister."

"When?"

This was going too far, but before I could hit her, she gathered her wits. "Arlette? I don't think she said. She didn't sound anxious or disturbed or anything. Just a Sunday call. Probably wants the answer to a clue."

One thing that Arlette and I have in common is a taste for cryptic crossword puzzles, and occasionally, rarely, we consult to complete the last clues in the Sunday *Star* puzzle. Now, Carole's suggestion became my excuse to call back. I guessed that Arlette had made an excuse to call me in case Carole was home, and I immediately started to feel crowded. Was this how it was going to be until Arlette cooled down or off?

"She's probably got it now. I'll wait, see if she calls back."

The phone rang and I jumped a real quarter of an inch. I picked it up. "I haven't done the crossword yet," I said. "I've been out and not even looked at it. Carole guessed you were calling about the crossword, though."

I hoped she would realize that this was a signal that Carole was in the room, so for Christ's sake don't get personal, but she could disguise what she wanted to say by pretending it was a clue.

Ginger said, "Crosswords are for wankers. Could I talk to Carole?"

"She's busy," I said. "She's looking out the window. What do you want her for?" My mind was still so taken up with the need to make my end of any telephone conversation banal, that I overlooked the rudeness of my question.

Before I could apologize, he said, "I want to get the recipe for her brownies. What the fook is it to you?"

"A recipe? A cookbook recipe, like?" I blundered on. Carole doesn't have any recipes and I had a job imagining that Ginger spent his Sundays filling the freezer with baked goods.

"Well, no, actually I want to know what you do with fertilizer if you want to blow up Robarts Library. Of course a cookbook recipe. What's the matter with you?"

"Sorry, I was daydreaming. Here." I handed the telephone to Carole. "Ginger," I said. "He thinks you're a cook." I was so relieved it wasn't Arlette I was getting light-headed. Carole doesn't mind admitting her limitations as a cook, but she doesn't like me making jokes about it to other people.

"Ginger," she said now, into the phone. "Hi. No. But I can find it. Call me tomorrow in the afternoon. I'll have it for you by then." She replaced the phone. "He wants to know how to make bacon-and-egg pie. I told him I'd find out and let him know."

"Quiche?"

"Bacon-and-egg pie. His grandmother used to make it. In Scunthorpe, before quiche crossed the Atlantic. Or Channel, I guess I mean. Or got that far north." She went back to staring out the window.

The phone rang again. I was remembering a joke I used to tell about a girl I met in Paris, an American from Texas who asked me, outside a restaurant, if I knew the French word for quiche, and wondering if I could adapt the joke to make the speaker a Scunthorpian, just as Arlette said, "When you get to it, tell me what the answer to twenty-four across is. I must see you to fill you in." She was calm, but I could swear she was suppressing something like hysteria, if you can actually suppress hysteria.

"No need," I said. "I'm not busy."

"Tomorrow afternoon. I'll cancel my appointments and come out to Hambleton."

"No. It doesn't fit. Try something else." How long could I keep this up? It was like simultaneously filling in one of those puzzles where there are two sets of clues, one cryptic, one regular.

"Then when? Where? I have to see you before you do something silly."

"Let me have a look at the puzzle," I said. What was she talking about? "I've got some essays to mark before I can get to it. Before dinner, though. Yes, I'll call you."

Carole looked away from the window. "Problem?"

"I should never have introduced Arlette to cryptic crosswords. She's like you, she doesn't have the gift, but unlike you she thinks she does and she's very competitive. Where will you find a recipe for bacon-and-egg pie?"

"For what? What do I want that for? Oh, right. There's a Welsh woman in the canteen in The Buildings. She'll know. She used to be a cook in an English grammar school before her son emigrated and she followed him out. She'll know, or she can phone her mother in Wales and find out." She returned to the window.

chapter twenty-six

I noticed that Carole had been behaving very slightly out of character lately; not all the time and not much, but her behaviour was not sliding along the accustomed grooves and I was experiencing a few very small surprises, bumps along the road of understanding. No more than that. Call it a mild pattern of evasiveness, consistent with her not wanting to talk about the fact that a medical examination had shown that she was going to have to stop reading for say, six months, to rest her retinas, and she was trying to decide what to do with her life.

Once before, about two years ago, Carole started to behave very oddly indeed, staring at me from the other side of the room when she thought I was asleep, that sort of thing. Actually, just that: I can't think of other examples like it, just a lot of staring. On that occasion she was worried that I was yielding to a private sexual obsession that I won't go into but was original enough to have been grounds for a divorce even for a Catholic and certainly felt to her like a threat to our own very ordinary and satisfactory life. Eventually she told me what it was all about, but after we had sorted it out we were left shaken, her by what she thought she had found out about me, and me by what

I realized she had believed about me, however briefly. We worked our way through it until the air between us was crystal clear, but it had been alarming.

These new vibes I was getting were nothing like that, creating just an off-key hum, but it was there. What I feared was that it was the result of her having got some odd vibes from me, or rather from Arlette, and she had wondered where they came from. I was worried because for all I knew Arlette was reckless, and I had to handle her so that not only my world with Carole didn't tremble, but also so that the two sisters didn't fall out.

I tackled the crossword. I was going to have to spend half an hour with it before I could make my next telephone call coherent, plausible, and message bearing. I got engrossed, of course, and spent most of the afternoon on it, but by the time I called Arlette back I had worked out a code. "It's collateral," I said. "The clue is 'I guarantee the hillside is safe'. 'Col' means 'hill', 'lateral' means 'side' and collateral is what you guarantee the safety of a loan with."

She said, "I was working on 'collarbone'. Is Carole there?"

"Yes. The thing is, 'collarbone' would upset twenty-two down."

"The whole corner is a mess. Look, think of something you have to buy, some grocery item, and let's bump into each other in the Loblaws at St. Clair and Bathurst. Can you get there at three?"

"Four. Something to do with wine, I would think." This was like charades.

"Good. Got it. I'll meet you in the liquor store at four and we'll go have coffee."

"That fits. Okay?" I hung up.

On Monday Masaka thanked me for dinner saying what a fine time she had had.

"Aye," Ginger said. "Brilliant." But he didn't put much life into it.

I had the happy thought that he had probably had a poor evening by his standards if he had been planning to get his hands on Masaka.

I had a tiny idea for the creative writing course. I gave them the assignment of finding what they considered to be the best opening to a short story by a famous writer. Today they were going to read these paragraphs and try to understand why they liked them. And then, collectively, we would try to find anything the paragraphs or the students' comments on them had in common so as to assemble a list of things an opening paragraph might, or could, or should do. I intended at the end of the hour to send them away to write a brief essay on what makes a good opening paragraph.

I had no ideas on the subject myself, but I had looked up 'openings' in a few handbooks on creative writing, so I knew how they talked about the topic. I was actually spending more time on this class in which I had no faith than I would have on preparing *King Lear* or *Paradise Lost*. Any teacher who in terrified despair labours to find something interesting to say about an unmanageable work, *Moby Dick*, for example, or Pope's "Essay on Criticism," finds that the seemingly fruitless work done to find anything to talk about has in fact filled his head with a mass of learned chaff that will do in the absence of a lecture and something real to say.

Today I was trying to develop the germ of an idea about how to teach, or at least get through, the course in a way I might be able to repeat next year. I decided that we would assemble our own text with chapters on the lines of our developing "Openings". After "Openings" we would move on to "Closing Paragraphs'", while I thought of other topics. Already they were coming through: "Introducing a Character", "'The Function of Description" and (a real one)

"What's Wrong with Adverbs". As soon as I thought of it, the list became endless and rich. The point, I thought, should be that each student should write his or her own text, clarifying for themselves what they were trying to do, and then maybe their exam would consist of writing the table of contents and the introduction to the text they had written ...

I was jerked awake by the silence. Monica was waiting for me to tell her what I thought of her opening paragraph, but I had been contendedly daydreaming about my idea. There was a time when I would have panicked at being caught out like that, and tried to fudge something to say from the scraps of sentences that had got through the fog, but I'm too old a hand for that now.

I looked at her, and waited another six seconds, count-ing, then said, smiling, "I'm sorry, Monica. Something you said right at the beginning got caught in an idea we were working on in the last class, and I missed most of your remarks. Would you mind going back to the beginning and letting us have it again?"

You can get away with that once a term with each class.

Back in the office I was in time to interrupt Masaka and Ginger yet again. Ginger had obviously been moving in on her and she just as clearly wasn't pleased. When I came through the door Ginger had got back to his desk, and Masaka looked like someone who had just received some not very welcome news, which I assumed was Ginger's proposition.

The psychologist put his head round the door, asking, "Litotes?"

"It's a form of meiosis," Masaka said without looking up.

Ginger and I nodded, then, when the psychologist had gone, turned to Masaka. "What's meiosis?" Ginger asked, ahead of me.

"It's a form of understatement. Not uncommon."

"I've never heard of it, " Ginger said.

"I mean, 'not uncommon' is an example of meiosis."

They went off to teach, and the phone rang. It was Berky. "All alone?" he asked.

What did he want? Then I remembered: he was assessing the threat to Masaka from Ginger. "Yes," I said.

"Are the others teaching?"

"They just left."

"Good. Well, then, I just called to say is that in my professional judgement you don't have to worry about Masaka Kinoshita. She has all the equipment she needs to protect her from the advances of the hairy ape, friend Ginger. She's as tough as he is horny and she will remain inscrutable to him or any other male not of her choosing."

"Good on you, Berky. This is really something. Makes me believe that psychiatry is something more than calling up a set of revealed codes."

"What are you talking about?"

"Just creating an analogue with my word processor. When the text is misbehaving—paragraphs indenting too far, that sort of thing—I press a key called 'Reveal Codes' and find all the instructions I've given it while I've been working on the document. Then I clean out the ones I no longer want and return to the text, like coming back into the daylight from the developing room. I've often thought that's what you shrinks do, you get the patient to lie down, press 'Reveal Codes' and see what instructions that the patient didn't know about are screwing up the text he now wants to create. But what you're saying is you've spent an evening with the main text and you're prepared to offer an opinion without going into 'Reveal Codes'."

"Not an opinion. I'm telling you in ordinary layman's English, that Masaka is in no danger from Ginger. You don't have the training to understand how I reached this conclusion, but you can trust me."

"I will. Her being oriental and inscrutable and all didn't get in the way of your analysis?"

He ignored this. "Now I'd better go. Do you all come back to the office between classes?"

"Not usually. The classes are inevitably in different buildings, and there isn't time."

"Right. Well, I'll be off, then."

"Thanks," I said. I was still slightly wary of him. A few minutes ago I was afraid that the call was somehow about Arlette, and there was still a little of that left. But it seemed we were on good terms. Pushing my luck, I said, "How's Arlette?"

He said, "You saw her on Saturday. Did she seem to have a cold or something?"

"Just being polite. I forgot who I was talking to."

"What do you mean?"

"Oh, Christ, Berky, *you* tell *me*."

I went off to find some coffee. I had one more class in which a student was going to comment on Robert Frost's "Acquainted With the Night", a soothing exercise if you've taught it as many times as I have. After that I could go back to my other lives.

chapter twenty-seven

I dropped in to the agency on my way downtown.

"I'll call her," my boss said. "Make a verbal report of it. So it's your opinion that his little bit of poontang is over and there's nothing more for you to watch for?"

"The landlord thinks so. He says the fact that the guy hasn't paid his rent means he's leaving. He's supposed to give a month's notice but the landlord thinks he'll just walk."

"I'll call her, then. In the meantime, make out your report." He picked up the paper condom packet by one corner as if the idea of condoms offended him. "I'll keep this in case she needs it. You'd better initial them, with the dates. What's this Ho-Ho-Ho stuff?"

"Turn it over."

He turned the packet over and read the other side, which was printed with the face of a pirate—head-scarf, eye-patch—and the words "The Jolly Roger".

"Funny thing to put on a packet of safes," he said. "Oh, I see." He burst into a roar. "I've never seen these in drugstores. Where would you get some?" He roared again. "You think they come in black?" He put it into an envelope and dropped it into the file he was keeping. "Nothing like that in Leaside. How about your neighbourhood?"

"Try the Condom Shack on Queen Street."

By the time I got home he had a reply for me. "She says it is most important that you stay on the job for at least another week. Play it by the book, Joe. I think she's up to something. I wouldn't be surprised if she isn't planning to confront him next Tuesday or Thursday, and make you witness. So don't *you* be surprised."

Now all I had to come was a chat with Arlette.

I would be no good at all at adultery—not this open marriage nonsense, but the old-fashioned kind where if you got caught your world would go down the chute like the sinners in a medieval church painting, you and everything you hold dear, the house, the baby carriage, your mutual funds (done symbolically with dollar signs), all jumbled up, feet in the air, falling to a place lit by flames and staffed by mothers-in-law with pitchforks, looking happy at last.

I've never been married and the only time I tried to keep two women in my life I was worn out in about three weeks with the strain of the deception. Besides, the idea of deceiving Carole has never entered my head. *L'homme moyen sensual*—that's me, an averagely horny male approaching middle age in a satisfying relationship. So even though I could explain having a tête-à-tête in another neighbourhood with Arlette more easily than I could, say, with Masaka, I still found myself constructing the answer to the question Carole might ask when a colleague of hers reports seeing me, etc.

First of all, I scanned the shelves of the liquor store for something unfamiliar and came up with Coleraine, an Irish whiskey new to me, which I hadn't seen in my local store, and which I could claim had been recommended to me by an Irishman in the History department. So that was one reason for being there, and bumping into Arlette. Another reason was that the car wash at St Clair and Bathurst was arguably as close to us as any other, and it was certainly time to get the van washed. And then the parking at Loblaws is free and we needed a couple of tongs worth of washed salad and a stick of bread to accompany the night's Alfredo sauce.

Put that lot together and I surely had a watertight excursion.

Arlette said, "Well, well. What are you doing here?"

I explained carefully so she would remember when she was interrogated. "And you?" I asked.

"This is where we shop," she said. "My office is just across St Clair."

Good for you, I thought. "Where's the coffee shop?"

She led the way and asked me to get her a decaf latte while she found a table. I ordered two.

"Now," she said. "My turn, okay. Don't interrupt. I've thought about what I want to say. No. Don't interrupt."

"But ..."

"Shut up! Now. I think you should restrict your references about Masaka in front of Carole to one a day."

We ate the foam in silence. I said, "And?" Get to the point, I meant.

"And nothing. That's it. I'm trying to tell you that at the moment you mention Masaka about ten times a day, and you should stop it before Carole starts screaming."

"Has Carole complained to you?"

"No. I'm taking it on myself."

"Just for Carole's sake?"

"Of course. What else?"

I said, after a pause, "I thought we were going to be talking about something else. I thought I had been getting some strong signals lately. From you. Nothing to do with Masaka."

"I realized that the other night. That's my fault, for getting curious about ..."

"Me? And Masaka?"

She paused for a long time. "Yes. In particular. And in general, too."

I thought about that. "Me in general?"

"Sort of. I wondered what made you tick."

I took a long time to think about my next remark, guessing that my chance of an easy exit depended on it. "And all this started just because you were worried about me and Masaka."

"About you and Carole, more importantly."

"So I'm wrong." I said finally. It would be hard for her to fault a *mea culpa*.

"If I've guessed right about what you mean, yes."

I took a deep breath. "You aren't obsessed with me."

"No."

"Christ. What a bloody fool I am."

"Now you are going to hate me," she offered. "Making you expose yourself."

"Let me think," I said, not absolutely certain what she was talking about, but welcoming her desire to share the responsibility for whatever had nearly derailed us. "No" I said.

"That's a relief."

"Isn't it. And now we've averted a major tragedy, at some cost to my ego—by the way my libido is fine: I was just trying to put you off ..."

"You did that, all right."

"But now, please, don't try to help out Carole and me any more until one of us asks."

"My intentions were good. I'm fond of you, you know."

"I believe it. Now let's move on, shall we?"

She was lying, I think, though that's a harsh word. But I was very keen to support her story, and grateful to her. I don't know what happened. My guess is that her libido started to play around, and then her professional self told her libido to knock it off.

She was wrong about me, though. Masaka is an enigma, and a very interesting one, but no threat to Carole.

We drank our coffee, smiling, sort of. In a minute, I thought, we'll be friends. We have shared a little bit of personal history that will stay private. I felt fond of her, no longer wary. I stood up and kissed her on the cheek.

"Are we pals still, then?" She folded her arms across her chest, pulling herself into a shell.

I punched her lightly on the shoulder and left.

chapter twenty-eight

On Tuesday night I parked in the usual spot and eyed the sausage vendor eyeing me. He waved. Some gumshoe, I am. When the light came on behind the blind and the silhouettes appeared, he waved again and pointed up to the window. I would like to have ignored him but he was not sure I had seen him or the silhouettes so he waved and pointed, and pointed and waved, and I had to open my door, stick my hand out, and wave back before he subsided. He was starting to draw a crowd.

Then I noticed something curious about the silhouettes: just before the light went out, one silhouette seemed much less animated than usual, as if it was a dummy. Normally they embraced with obvious animation but tonight they pecked once, hugged briefly, and turned out the light. When the light came back on, much sooner than usual, I saw why I had registered an oddness about them. Tyler was the same as always, but his lover's profile, specifically her hairstyle, had changed radically. The back hair was a couple of inches longer than it had been the previous week. And you could see the circle of a necklace made with big chunky stones, which I had never seen before. Now I could see why Mrs. Tyler want-

ed me to stay on the job; as she had suspected, Tyler was
bonking more than her sister.

What I needed now to complete my report was one more
picture, a picture of this woman, preferably framed in the
doorway of the building to identify her and the location. At
dusk, a single light bulb in a wire cage came on over the
side door and burned all night, so I would have no problem
getting some kind of image. Normally in this business, you
take your pictures from inside the car, inconspicuously, but
I was going to have to get over and find a spot to hide in it.

I put my camera in my pocket, waited until the sausage
vendor was busy—he was still looking at me and grinning
in the intervals between customers like a half-witted
bystander in a newsreel shot, no more than a nuisance, but
there was the risk that if he saw me leave the car he might
shout and wave.

I scuttled across the street behind his back and disappeared, I hoped, into the alley that ran past the side entrance
of Glinka's building. I found what I wanted immediately, a
compound holding garbage cans, fenced with trellis six feet
high. The holes in the trellis offered plenty of room for my
camera, and I didn't even have to crouch to hide.

It didn't take them long to get dressed. Tyler and his
woman appeared more or less together and spent a few minutes discussing which way to go until finally he came down
the alley and turned to walk away, while she spent a moment
touching her costume here and there the way women do, and
walked out on to the street, all of which gave me plenty of
time to take a dozen pictures of the two of them as well as
her on her own, underneath the lamplight.

I followed her out to the street and turned right behind
her onto Dundas, and then another curious thing happened. She turned right again at the end of the block,
down the side street, where Tyler was waiting to pick her

up in his yellow Volvo. Just for my own benefit, I got two more pictures of her getting into the car, including one of the licence plate, before they drove off.

Full of things to think about, I walked back to my car where my friend the sausage vendor was waiting for me. "Got her, eh?" he said. "You saw them up there? Just a quickie they had this time, eh? Want a sausage?" He winked three times, grinned, and moved his feet as if to perform a two-step.

Then I lost it. I was offended that this street merchant should feel free to talk about the woman he believed I loved with such easy coarseness, and to my face, yet. "Why don't you stick your sausage up your ass and fuck off?" I said.

As soon as I said it I realized I would have to avoid him in future, park where I could watch the window, and stay out of his line of vision. But that wasn't a serious consequence, because I had only one more night on watch, and I could handle that. No, my mistake was that I had finally made an enemy of the bastard, which was self-indulgent and stupid, and could have caused me a lot of trouble.

chapter twenty-nine

"There's something weird going on," I said to the boss the next morning. I explained what I thought was slightly odd about the image behind the blind the night before. "I'm sure we are being set up," I said. "I need back-up."

"Who do you think we are, the Mounties? There's no money for back-up. This is the last night. All you have to do is watch the window, and report what you see. No back-up, nothing like that. What do you mean, anyway, back up?"

"I want to get closer," I said. "I want to be by the door when they arrive, and when they leave. I need to get a good look at the sister."

"So go over to Queen Street. Have lunch at one of her tables."

"No, I mean ..." and then I thought, Why not? "I'll do that, and get back to you."

"I just need a report that you watched Tyler. Okay? That's what she's paying for."

I turned my attention back to my main source of income.

As far as I could tell, Ginger still had Masaka in his sights, because whenever I arrived in the office the two of them were silent, obviously having just resumed marking papers or whatever they were supposed to be doing. I assumed that by now Masaka had learned how to handle him.

Ginger had become rather still, and somewhat sad. The days when I had surprised him *in flagrante* seemed long gone, and I guessed he was simply enduring a stalemate. I tried joking with him, asking him about the conquests of yesteryear, but he was neither embarrassed nor entertained by my chaff, though he politely twisted one side of his face in a rictus of pseudo-amusement, acknowledging the sally while letting it bounce off him. Suddenly, he said, "Do you play chess?"

"What?"

"Chess. I thought we might have a game."

"I haven't played chess since I was fourteen. You at a loose end?"

"Not especially. Does Carole?"

"What, play chess? I've no idea. The question's never cropped up. She hates Scrabble, I can tell you that." I had an idea. "Never mind chess. You free tonight?"

"Apart from this." He pointed to the mound of essays.

Ginger knows what I do to augment my income, but we don't talk about it. My colleagues generally think I work as some kind of security guard and are slightly embarrassed by the idea. But, sharing an office with me, Ginger has necessarily heard my end of conversations I have with Jack Atkinson, my boss. So I have let him in on the truth that, though "Private Detective" would be stretching it a bit, I am more of an investigator than a guard. He understands, too, why I no more want to advertise how I moonlight than I would if I were working nights for an escort agency.

"I need someone to help me watch someone," I said. I explained the situation as concisely as I could. "I need someone to sit in the car with my cap on while I stay free. Someone to impersonate me."

"To do what?"

"Follow him, if he goes for a walk."

"If he goes for a ride? What then?"

"I'll think of something. Will you do it?"

He considered, but he looked cheerful at the idea. "Sure. Let's hope he's up to something. Might be a lark. What time will you pick me up? Shall I pack a rod?"

We agreed on a time, and I went off to class.

Richard lay in wait for me when I returned from a class where I had nattered on about the importance of reading your essays aloud, of getting someone else to read them back to you, of taping your reading and theirs and listening to them back to back, all of which I believed in sincerely.

Richard steered me to the caféteria and bought me coffee. I said, "I have to be downtown by twelve-thirty."

He said, "What have you heard?"

"No real change," I said. "Daniels has five votes and Jenkins has six. You and Riddell have two votes each, including your own. And still three 'don't knows'."

"What about the sessionals?"

"You mean how do they feel about you? I don't know how to answer that question. We aren't lined up behind banners like you people. Because we don't have a vote, we haven't bothered to sort out how we feel. It doesn't matter, does it?"

"It might if there's a deadlock and a second round of voting. If everything depended on one vote then how the sessionals felt could influence things."

"All a bit vague, Richard. I mean ..."

"Listen," he said, looking round. "I think the sessionals ought to have more influence than they've got now."

"They couldn't have less."

"I think the sessionals *ought* to have some voting power. It seems to me quite wrong that more than a third of the teaching staff should be totally disenfranchised. I don't mean full voting rights, but ..."

"Richard," I interrupted him.

"What?"

"Stick it up your ass. You didn't just think of this. What are you up to?"

"I think it would be appropriate and fair if the sessionals had some form of proportional vote in relation to their workload. I've been doing the sums; if you add up all the hours the sessionals and part-timers teach, it comes to six and a bit full-time workloads. Now it seems to me only fair, that being the case, that the sessionals collectively should have, say—three votes. Never mind the bit."

"Why not six?"

"In theory, of course. But I'm trying to be pragmatic. Historically, the right to vote always came in gradually. You know, first the householder, then all men over twenty-five and so on until the women get the vote. If you move too fast it frightens people."

"And would they vote in pieces? Like, would I register my three-fifths or whatever I get, all to you? Or could I spread it around, a fifth here, two-fifths there, that sort of thing?"

"You could try to take it seriously, for a start."

"I can't, Richard, because it's bullshit. What do you plan to do to win these three and a bit votes to your side?"

"I was counting on your support, not just the vote but in the campaign."

"It's tricky, isn't it? I mean, there are no votes among the sessionals at the moment, so I can't start tomorrow going around shouting, 'Vote for Costril and equal rights, rah, rah, rah.' You would be in favour of equal rights, would you, for the sessionals, once some of us get a piece of the vote? I mean, that would be the next step, wouldn't it?"

I thought my question was rhetorical, but he paused. "Up to a point," he said.

I started to scream immediately. "Up to a *point*? Up to a fucking *point*? What does that mean? You had ten years of day labouring before your present sinecure, and you answer 'Up to a point'. I should tell you where to go."

"No, no. I just mean, yes, we are in agreement on the principle of equal rights, but we should adopt the principle in a manageable fashion."

"Manageable for who? Not for the poor bastards who are managing on half pay at the moment. Right? You were there. What do you say?"

I must say I was enjoying myself. Soon we would find common ground, but right now it was good to have someone to belabour about the injustices the college inflicts on the sessionals, someone who knows about it as well as I do. And whatever game he was up to he knew that this was the only issue that mattered to me and my kind. He couldn't dodge it.

"Look," he said. He wasn't actually sweating but he certainly was getting a bit of a shine. "Look," he said again, confirming his unease. "Let's agree that in principle I am all for equal rights."

"And you will say so, publicly."

"Up to a point."

I laughed. He had clearly forgotten where the phrase came from, and what it really meant. "Will you or won't you?"

"I will give it my support, but I must qualify it."

"How?"

"We just don't know all the implications yet. I mean, let's start with tenure. If everyone has tenure and the college suffers a decline in enrolment, who should, say, take a year's leave of absence? The most senior member of faculty? The most junior?"

"We worked all that out, you and I. All the sessionals want is to be dealt with fairly, like steelworkers, say. New people would be on probation for a year, two if you like, and then be given tenure, or be asked to leave. And as for your question, we'll live with the principle, 'Last hired, soonest fired'. It's a return to the old days, if you like, before the single criterion for staffing a university was how little cash you could do it for. It simply should not be possible to keep people on staff for years at half the pay of their colleagues and no benefits. Remember? Remember saying that?"

Richard knew we were at the sticking point. "All right. It will be part of my platform. Equality in principle, and in pay and benefits now."

"Tenure offered as appropriate?"

"Yes."

"No 'up-to-a-point' bullshit?"

"No."

I nodded and breathed slowly. It was odd and disconcerting to find myself suddenly as angry with Richard as he had taught me to be with the rest of them, but it proved to me that the core dispute was not a fiction. I tried to get some perspective back. "I think I can swing that," I said. "But, let's say I can carry the part-timers, what difference does it make? Who will care? Because you may be able to stir up some shit, but I can't believe you'll get votes for the working classes overnight."

"I've got a couple of weeks." He stood up, looking satisfied.

I wondered what was in his mind. In days gone by he would have confided in me but this conversation confirmed that a significant shift had taken place in our relationship. Whatever 'up-to-a-point' might mean, it was the remark of a dodger and it indicated that Richard was no longer reacting instinctively in the interests of his old mates, but considering the merits of the case from a new standpoint, that of someone with tenure.

I realized then that much as I had enjoyed fighting the good fight with Richard by my side, I didn't like him and never had. I had never invited him home, for example, because we had nothing in common. In order to agree on the main injustice, we had papered over the normal disagreements that might have revealed our lack of affinity—his hostility towards Northrop Frye (whom he didn't understand), for instance; my distaste for E.M. Forster (the subject of his long brooded over doctoral thesis), a novelist whose disfiguring elitism renders his stories implausible as far as I am concerned. But only once did we come to a crisis: when I suggested that W.H.Auden was more pastichist than poet, and I thought he was going to hit me. Still, my discovery of the new Richard shouldn't interfere with his plans. Misery had made strange bedfellows of us once, I saw now, and henceforth politics would perform the same office.

chapter thirty

It was time now to sort out the riddle of the book-seller's women.

That there were two women, closely related, in Tyler's life, I had evidence and no doubt, and until Tuesday night it had not been a problem. Tyler was bonking his wife's sister, was all. The similarity had reminded me of that priest who laid out ten no-no rules for detective stories, one of them being that you must not have your puzzle depend on the mis-identifying of twins. I had never thought much of Father Knox's rules, and anyway, this was life, not fiction. And also, until now the striking likeness of the two women had only made me aware of the identity of the woman behind the blind. Now, though, the plot had doubled and I wanted to look at its elements more closely.

I got a picture of the sister without much trouble as I shuffled about in front of Le Clochard, once more imitating a photographer putting together a streetscape. It was a beautiful day and still not quite noon when she came skipping along the sidewalk, a bit late, probably, and I caught her as she paused in the doorway to speak to a waiter who was having a smoke before the lunch hour rush began. And then I heard a conversation that froze my blood. The owner of the restaurant appeared in the doorway, kissed the sister on the top of the head and said, "How's it now?"

She looked up at him, gave him a kiss on the cheek in return, and said, "There was never anything wrong with it. Just you, panicking."

"Your whole eyeball was bloodshot. I couldn't let you scare the customers away. Let's have a look." He took her head between his hands and rotated it slowly, peering into her eye. "Nothing there now. Did they take long?"

"Did they take long? About two minutes. But to get my two minutes I had to sit in the bloody emergency ward from five-thirty until eight o'clock. I was afraid to read, even, in case I went blind."

"What did the doctor call it?"

"A broken blood vessel. He promised me it would be fine tomorrow." She dropped the cigarette on the sidewalk, kicked it away towards the gutter, and went inside to start work.

Well, well. I hardly needed the photos now. The 'other woman', Tyler's sister-in-law, had not been near the love nest the night before. So who did I take pictures of? Another sister? Triplets? Father Knox would never allow that.

Tyler's wife was harder to get, but I still wanted pictures of them both at roughly the same time to prove they were different people, and not one female quick-change artist, and I waited across the street from the bookstore for an hour and a half before she came out. But I could testify that no one had entered the store since I left Le Clochard, so this one could not be the waitress, and I got a couple of good shots of her looking up at the sky giving the profile that I needed. I took the film into a camera shop on the block and ordered their famous one-hour service, to be picked up on the way home.

I galloped across Toronto, listened to two students relate (their term) to the speaker in Marvell's "To His Coy

Mistress", and galloped back downtown. I collected the pictures from the camera shop and drove home to compare and contrast them.

I hardly needed to set them out on the kitchen table; I could see immediately that it was a case of a powerful likeness but not of twins. I laid out in a row the pictures of Mrs. Tyler I had taken. Below them I put a row of pictures of the waitress "sister" (whether she was a sister or a cousin or just a lookalike didn't matter to the thread I was unravelling). Underneath I put another row of Mrs. Tyler, and then took out all the full-face shots, leaving only the profiles. It wasn't hard to see. You might have been surprised by the resemblance in the full-face pictures, even wondered if it was the same person with slightly rearranged hair, or different make-up; but in profile it was clearly two different women. A slightly indented nose on Mrs. Tyler, a sharper jawbone on her sister, laborious to describe but very easy to point out when they were enlarged. I had no doubt that Tyler was apparently having an affair with both his wife and his sister-in-law, which was absurd but maybe some kind of kinkiness I hadn't caught up with. Time would tell.

I pondered how much of this should go in my report. I had been hired to observe a single window that had framed the amorous embraces of Tyler and a woman that the wife wanted to know about. I extracted the pictures that told that story, leaving the rest to solve some future puzzle, something along the lines of that French movie *Diabolique*. Then I wrote a report detailing what I had found, including the contraceptive envelope, which would be pretty conclusive when my client decided to make her move, and put the whole thing in a large envelope to be checked by my boss before my client picked it up.

chapter thirty-one

"**W**here's the evidence that Ginger is trying to seduce Masaka?"

Carole and I were chatting while we were waiting for the dinner to heat up. We were trying a new take-out place in Hazelton Lanes that looked like an adequate replacement for the much-mourned Marks and Spencers.

"He's gone very quiet. You remember how active he was when he arrived; there was the Assistant Dean of Continuous Learning ..."

"I know, I know all about them," she said, irritably, I thought, leading me to remember that Carole is not interested in other people's lives; she dislikes gossip. "But there has been no sign of women around for months, right?"

"Two, at least."

"Then I expect you're right; it's Masaka."

"You think I ought to warn her?"

Carole exploded with something between a laugh and a shriek. "Who do you think you are?" she yelped. "How old is Masaka? Thirty? Even in Japanese, that's grown up. Mind your own business." And then she slammed into the kitchen and set about collecting the implements and dishes to defrost the dinner. These were bad signs and I shut up, but not without wondering why her reaction mightn't have been a shade lighter.

We ate quickly because Carole was still in a huff. I collected my camera and got ready to go. "This is my last night on this job," I said.

"This the horny bookseller?"

I told her about the odd case of the lookalike women.

"I expect you're imagining things again," she said.

"There *are* two women, and they look alike."

"So you say." She returned to her book. "Don't wake me up when you come in."

Of all the farewell remarks that are exchanged between consenting adults, that is the one I like least.

I picked up Ginger and told him as much as I knew myself about what was going on. As far as Mrs. Tyler was concerned I was simply doing as I was told, but there was something else going on, of that I felt sure. This was the last night and I didn't know why even this was necessary. Whatever she was up to, everything she needed was already in the report. The mystery of the photos I parked in the back of my brain. But I wasn't imagining anything.

This time I parked half a block away, behind a U-Haul van which blocked the sausage vendor's view of us but still allowed me to watch the window, and someone in the room to see my car. For all I knew she was planning to confront Tyler later that night and wanted me there, taking notes, to back her up with my report.

Tyler parked his yellow Volvo down the alley and ten minutes later the light came on in the window, and they were embracing, and no more than two or three minutes after that the light went out. I stayed where I was for want of anything better to do.

I said to Ginger, "Just to be sure, can you drive?" You can never tell with English immigrants. Anyone over the age of sixteen from Bosnia or Qtar or Turkey can handle anything with four wheels, or with four legs and a hump, for that matter, but young Englishmen get weaned from their bicycles much later.

"Why? You all wore out? Yes, I can drive. And I've got a licence. My dad made me get one before I left Scunthorpe, and it's still valid. Dad had a cousin, house painter, came over here, couldn't keep a job because he couldn't take his ladders on the buses in the rush hour."

"Surely that would be the same in Scunthorpe?"

"He could manage on his bike there, carrying the ladders on his shoulder and hanging the tin of paint from the handlebars. But it's hard to cycle up to Newmarket with a ladder on your shoulder. Take you a couple of days, too, wouldn't it? Besides, you wouldn't be allowed on the 401."

"You having me on?"

"No, but I think my dad might have been. He was a wag. You do much of this?"

"Surveillance?"

"Peeping Tom."

"This is my first case."

"You wouldn't want many, would you? A dirty business."

"Once upon a time, this is what most private detectives did. You needed the evidence for a divorce."

"You must be glad they changed the law."

"Even then, a lot of the evidence was faked, which, I just realized, is what I think we're doing."

"Faking evidence?"

"Right. Hey, that's a real quickie." Tyler was coming out the side door of the building already. He walked over to his car, and I congratulated myself on my instincts. I hadn't made sense of the events so far and here was one more unexplained act. "Stay there," I said.

I got out of the car and followed Tyler down the street

until he got in his car and started up. I ran back and found a cab in time to give the driver the usual order.

We didn't have far to go. The Volvo was heading to the shop. Tyler got out and disappeared into the alley behind the building as I paid off my cab. I was just in time to watch him let himself into the back door. The light on the ground floor was switched on; I crouched down under the window and for the next fifteen minutes I watched Tyler unsystematically dump his merchandise from the shelves on to the floor. When he had made enough of a mess, he turned to the safe, unlocked it in a few seconds, withdrew three or four books and put them carefully into a haversack, and finally lifted out what looked liked a briefcase. After that, he turned out the lights and I scurried around the side of the building as he came out the back door. There was just enough light for him to glance up and down the alley for any sign of strangers, turn, and with a swift upraised leg, kick in the door to simulate a "break-and-enter," and walk quickly back to his car, the briefcase under his arm.

I ran and found a cab to take me back to my car, where Ginger was waiting. He reported that the Volvo had arrived and Tyler was now in Glinka's building.

As he was telling me, the light came on in Tyler's love nest, Tyler and one of his women embraced, and that was that.

Ginger said, "She turned the light on and paraded behind the blind while you were away, opening her arms like Hedy Lamarr in that nudie flick. Just for a minute."

"Long enough for you to observe her."

"Plenty of time for that. Can I go now?"

"I'll take you home."

"No need. This is where the action is. I've been watching them go by. Not all in pairs, either. See you later." He got out of the car and strolled towards the sound of music and the glow of neon, farther south.

chapter thirty-two

I had actually started my engine when Tyler and one of the women came out of the building arm-in-arm and walked over to the Volvo. I watched them stop, embrace, and kiss. Tyler opened the back door of his car and threw in the briefcase and the backpack. She caught him as he turned and they kissed again before walking past my car. They stopped in front of the Matador restaurant, but moved on, apparently in search of the ideal dinner.

My job was done. From across the street I got one last picture of them looking at the menu outside a Spanish restaurant, and decided to leave them to it. I could see the Volvo down the side street, and I daydreamed a little, remembering the time I had had my pocket picked on the Madrid subway and wondering, If you threw a good-looking briefcase in the back of an unlocked car in Madrid, how long it would take for a shadow to detach itself from the wall and absorb the briefcase?

What happened, in fact, was just that, if one allows for the difference between a shadowy Madrid thief, and a fairly substantial Toronto street person scanning the street for someone with some spare change. He noted Tyler's carelessness, shuffled over to the Volvo as smartly as his broken boots would allow, retrieved the briefcase and the books, and scurried off as quickly as he could, not even bothering to shut the door of the car.

Full of instinct, I was out of the car and following him down the street as he, still moving, fumbled with the briefcase catch and got it open. In his Scott Mission hand-me-downs, searching through the briefcase, he looked like Red Skelton doing one of his Freddie-the-Freeloader sketches, a parody of a Bay Street lawyer, late for a meeting and searching for his copy of the agenda.

He ducked down an alley and stopped under a streetlight beside a dumpster. First he opened the briefcase and took out the packet of paper, then threw the parcel into the dumpster. The books took him a moment longer; he took one out, smelled it, then put it back in the haversack and threw the whole thing into the dumpster. He tucked the empty briefcase under his arm, and shuffled off.

These bins come in different sizes, and this one came to just over my head. There was a ledge on the side of the bin about halfway up, and I was able to hoist myself on to the lip and balance with my feet off the ground. You could say I was lucky because the dumpster was nearly full, so the top layer was very accessible, just under my nose. Do you know what people throw in those bins, apart from dog shit, I mean?

The package was resting on the top layer of crud and I was able to grab it by a cleanish corner and bring it out without tearing it. The bag of books was beginning to sink but I grabbed a strap and hauled it out as I swung my feet down on to the ground.

I tapped the bag on the side of the bin to dislodge a banana peel, and wiped the rest off with my sleeve. An old lady who had been watching me from the end of the alley came forward now and gave me a dollar. "Now you go to the mission on Spadina," she said. "They'll give you some nourishing soup and some clean clothes."

I looked down. I was wearing a pair of chinos and an old sweater, and some tennis shoes that I keep for fishing because they grip slippery rocks well and it doesn't matter if they get wet.

I took the dollar and thanked her, and when she had gone away, I read the covering sheet of the package under the lamplight at the end of the alley. There it was: "The Hemingway Papers". I lifted the cover and read half a sheet of the text, a story about two guys carrying a canoe through the woods into an inland lake. There was the beginning of a style, and on the way to that style there were handwritten corrections in a script that should be easy to identify.

Once, in a museum in England, I had suddenly come on to the manuscript of Keats's "Ode to a Nightingale" at a time when I had just finished reading Keats's letters and decided that, given a choice, I would much rather have known Keats than Wordsworth. Seeing that manuscript, discovering it for myself, as it were, I was afflicted with a weakness and had to sit down to avoid fainting. The sensation was momentary but blinding while it lasted. Nothing so powerful happened to me beside the dumpster, reading the first few sentences of the Hemingway Papers, but I had to get a clear signal from my heart that it was ready to start again before I could move.

I trotted off to my car where I had a sports bag for my tennis gear, put the manuscript down the side of the bag, zipped the bag shut, put it on the floor out of sight, the haversack next to it, and drove home. I had no idea what to do next, but I knew it would come to me. I could wait. It was clear I had stumbled into Tyler's other world, his night-time world, so to speak, and I would have to be careful to stay out of his way while I waited to see what he did when he found the manuscript was missing. In the meantime, I had a lot to attend to.

Auden wrote about the way ordinary life goes on in the interstices of scenes of great suffering, citing the "torturer's horse scratching its innocent behind on a tree" during the questioning of a heretic. I felt something of that in the next few days as my little dramas played themselves out while Hemingway's papers lay on a shelf in the apartment, next to Carol's printing supplies.

I had run through all the usual hiding places and settled on the full view gambit. Carefully unsealing a two-hundred-sheet pack of copy paper, I had removed enough sheets to create the space I wanted, then filled the gap with Hemingway, laid some copy paper on top, and resealed the pack with a touch of paste. Then (my masterstroke) I had torn open the pack at the top, and left it like that, for all the world a nearly full pack of paper which had just been opened. I distributed the inch-thick pad of paper that was left over, half of it in the rack of Carole's printer, the rest under a paperweight by my laptop, where it looked entirely innocent.

I left a part of my brain free to work on the problem of who the papers belonged to. Presumably Tyler, who had bought the stock from Curry, had first claim, but if that was the case, why hadn't he exercised it, and simply put the papers up for sale. And how and why had they surfaced after three years?

The owner of the Gresham would certainly make a claim. He would say that though he received a thousand in compensation, this was because he agreed the papers had disappeared for good, and Curry had just given him the money to get him off his back. Now the papers had reappeared, they were his. I wondered about Curry's widow. She could certainly cobble together an oral affidavit that her dead husband had paid a thousand for the right to own the papers personally, and he had never regarded them as part of the stock, nor included the loss for tax purposes.

They were among his private possessions and so belonged to her, his heir. I decided right then that I wanted her to be right, but I knew that Tyler would swindle her if he could.

That night I suffered the most acute teaching anxiety dream I have ever experienced. I've had enough of these dreams to handle the routine ones without much stress. They usually arrive on Sunday night in the form of a vision of myself, naked, on stage, the curtain up and the realization on my part that I haven't learned my lines. These dreams are common in the trade: I knew an old academic once who was still getting them fifteen years after he had retired. This particular dream had never come my way before and it took me five minutes of sitting up in bed, with the light on, to get over it.

Essentially, Fred, our chairman, was questioning me as to why I had not marked my students' exam papers, none of them, not ever. Apparently a student from ten years ago had decided to appeal his grade and a routine investigation had uncovered the fact that I had submitted a flawless-looking set of grades, but quite clearly without opening the exam booklets. Of course, I had given the good students good grades because I knew who they were, but in some cases, where the students had written an answer that was either very good or very bad, the grade bore no relation to it. So they checked back, and saw that I had never in my entire career bothered to mark an exam.

I sat there, sweating, waiting for it not to be true, and when Carole turned on her light I was more or less recovered, but still not sure of the source of my fear.

The radio provided some enlightenment. On *What's Up in the Arts* we heard about a break-in of a bookstore the night before. Jason Tyler, the owner, was still assessing the extent of the robbery, but he could confirm that the thieves had cleaned out his safe.He had lost four valuable books, worth fifteen thousand dollars, and an important manuscript that had just been discovered among the store's records, a manuscript that Tyler was in the process of having evaluated before he announced the find. The radio announcer added that when Tyler's bookstore was owned by his predecessor, it had been the scene of an almost identical robbery twenty years before, when documents known as The Hemingway Papers had been stolen during a break-in and never recovered.

Tyler confirmed that the papers that had been stolen last night looked very much like those that went missing twenty years ago, leading to the probability that they had never been stolen, but lost.

"So there it is," I said to Carole. "Now I know it all. I've spent the last three weeks creating an alibi for that guy; Ginger and I can both confirm that when his store was being broken into, he was apparently with his mistress in his pad on College Street. Unfortunately for him, I can also confirm that I was there watching him break into his own store. And when he realizes that, he's going to kill me."

"What are you going to do about it?"

"Nothing, yet."

"Then he'll get away with it."

"Not with the loot. I've got that." I told her the story of the thief and the dumpster.

"What are you going to do with it? This manuscript."

"Hand it over to the cops, eventually. But I'd like to be sure who owns it first."

"You know what you're doing?"

"Not altogether." I told her about the dream.

"What do you think that means?"

"That I'm shit scared, and I might get caught."

"Who by?"

"Tyler, I think."

"I'm calling the police."

"No! Give me a little while to think about it. I'd like to make up my mind who owns the papers first."

"Go to the police. Now."

chapter thirty-three

It would be too much to say that the college or even the division was abuzz with excitement, but the department had received a bit of news that generated a powerful hum along our corridors.

"What's the Faculty Council?" Ginger wanted to know after I had given him a summary of the action he had missed by heading down to the fleshpots the night before. To do so, I had had to tell him pretty well the whole story of the Papers.

He was impressed. "So these papers are at your house now?" he asked.

"Yes."

"And the books?"

"They are still in the van," I said.

"I'd find somewhere a bit more special than that if I were you," he said. "What are you going to do now, apart from telling the coppers, of course. You know there might be real money involved with this lot, and somebody could come after you with intent to maim."

"I know. I'm not sure what I'm going to do," I said.

He grinned. "Don't get nobbled. Now, tell me about this Faculty Council."

I asked him why he wanted to know.

"Some tosser on the phone was asking me if you approved what they're up to. Who's 'they'? This Faculty Council."

I settled into my chair, trying to forget that there was a pot of gold, literary and real, on my desk at home, so I could get on with my teaching. Ginger's question helped to distract me, and I explained.

The Faculty Council is an elected body which has to approve any changes in college affairs that might affect the faculty. In practice, it argues about the curriculum. The debates are always conducted in terms of what constitutes the ideal program for the students, but the not-so-hidden-agenda is about what constitutes the ideal program for the faculty.

Some years ago, for instance, it became apparent that Hambleton should catch up with the rest of the world and abolish compulsory physical education, a one-course requirement for getting a degree. Nerds hated the course, and since the Arts faculty especially was largely composed of people who had themselves been nerds as undergraduates they got a lot of sympathy.

Eventually, someone from the Geography department found a brilliant solution, proposing that physical education remain compulsory, but for the college not the student. That is, it would continue to be offered, and assigned some hours on the students' timetable, but the students were free to ignore it if they wanted. The students as a body did ignore it, preferring to have the hour off, and within two years the option disappeared.

"Is it self-governing? I mean, do they actually make the laws about the curriculum?" Ginger asked.

"Recommendations, which the Board of Governors can turn into laws if it wants. See, the Board has the money; it can do what it likes. The Faculty Council just recommends." I then spent ten minutes running through the various councils in the college, their powers, and how they are constituted.

I asked him who was the "tosser" who had called.

"Someone called Dennis Campbell. Sounded official. Who's he?"

"The president of the part-time and sessional Faculty Association. The PTSFA."

"Our union?"

"Our association. It's not a professional union."

"That right? Gentlemen songsters are we? Fucking rip-off more like it. Campbell wants to know what you're up to."

"Me?"

Ginger looked at a piece of paper on his desk. "He has been asked if the association supports the motion that the Faculty Association—the real pros, right?—has had placed on its agenda by Richard Costril. Is that the wanker used to sit in this chair? Aye, then. Campbell wants to know what it's all about."

"So what is it all about? All news to me."

"I asked Fred. He knew about it. Everyone round here has heard by now. Seems your pal Costril has put forward a motion that future chairmen of departments should be elected with the participation of all faculty, including part-timers, who should be counted as electors according to the value of their workload. What's it mean? Sounds like Costril's championing the people."

I laughed. "Sounds like he's up to something, more like. You might get half a vote yet. Who would you vote for?"

"I suppose right now, out of sheer gratitude and not because I like the bugger, it would have to be Costril."

"There you are, then. Add up all the bits and pieces of part-timers and assume our gratitude and it's Richard for king."

Ginger broke into song, to the tune of "O Tannenbaum"

(or "The Red Flag"). "The tenured class can kiss my ass, I've got the bleeding vote at last."

"The timing's good," I said. "He might have the college over a barrel. They'll have to delay our election until this gets debated and voted on, and then if it's passed Richard wins, and if it's thrown out it'll be the last straw. I mean the tenured faculty will be on one side and everybody else on the other, ours, including the administration and the Board of Governors because they don't care much about little things like who gets to be department chairman. There's nothing at stake as far as they are concerned, no money and no power. When the Faculty Association realize this they might see they are in trouble, because they won't want to be seen protecting jobs for the boys, their boys. Clever. So what's our chairman saying?"

"Dick? He thinks the idea has merit."

"Christ! That's it, then. When someone up above says an idea has merit—did he use that phrase?—it means he's all for it and wants it to happen if he can get away with it, but he's not sure if the time is ripe."

The door opened. Field, a part-timer who specialized in remedial English, stood in the doorway. "There's a meeting of the odds and sods in Room 403 at eight tomorrow morning. It's the only time we are all free."

He disappeared, and we heard him a few moments later making the announcement to John Wheeler and Frances Partridge, along the corridor.

"You going?" Ginger asked.

"I think we have to, don't you?"

"You don't think they'll be taking pictures of us as we go in?"

"Probably. Watch out for any janitor who isn't Portuguese."

chapter thirty-four

I had one of the more fluent female students read Hal's "I-know-you-all" speech and tell us what she thought the prince was up to. You have to do a bit of casting against gender if you want to involve the women in the class because there are only three female parts, none of them with much juice, and none in the scenes I wanted to talk about.

I chose a pretty Greek student to avoid any implication that I was asking her because of some masculine streak I saw in her. Quite the reverse, in fact: I was risking the opposite charge that I chose her because she sat in the front row, under the lectern, from where I could see down nine-tenths of her olive loveliness when she sat forward to scratch her ankle.

She read it well, sounding a bit as if she could play Joan of Arc in a year or two, and I got away with what was essentially a high school lesson. I'm going to have to dazzle them next week with a college type lecture, like they've seen in the movies, and for which I will claim that the two readings we've done have been preparation. Probably the mousetrap scene between Hal and his old man.

I had lunch with Richard, a BLT in a greasy spoon by the bus stop.

I said, "If this is your idea of 'secret', I would avoid espionage as a career, if I were you. It isn't beyond the bounds of possibility that a colleague will appear, looking for a quiet place to prepare a class while he's eating his sandwich, and you and I will look like plotters."

"So we are, at least I am. I need your help. I wanted to tell you how I read the latest development and see your reaction."

"Go ahead."

"I'm working on the theory that in a community like ours, all rumours are true, and there has been a rumour that the Board is considering my idea of giving the sessionals a say in the election. I heard they think the idea has merit. What do you think?"

I didn't want to share my insight into the phrase "has merit" with Richard yet. He obviously felt none of the portents in the words, the signs that something was about to happen.

I said, "Of the possibility that it's true? I think that's plausible."

"I want you to leak it, Joe, leak the possibility that it might be on the cards." He leaned on the table, agitated, watching my face for a sign of consent.

"Why 'leak'? It isn't secret, is it? I don't think you can have a secret rumour, can you? It's sort of contradicts itself."

"You mean like an oxymoron?"

"That's the word I was trying to avoid, because it isn't quite, is it? Maybe it is, but anyway, like Joe Kennedy said about the stock market when the elevator operator started asking him for tips, it's time to drop the word oxymoron before we find it in beer ads. The other day ..."

"For Christ's sake, fuck the other day, and oxymorons, too. Could we get back to my campaign? I want you to make sure that the department's aware of this rumour."

"Why?" I wasn't thinking about Richard much, just with the tenth of my mind I had left over from worrying about Tyler, and panicking about Arlette.

"Because it's *my* idea, for Christ's sake. If the sessionals like it, and they must, they'll give me credit for introducing it and give their bits of votes to me. Will you do it?"

"We don't have a lot of time. I have to be downtown by three, and you want these people clued in before eight o'clock tomorrow morning."

"Why? What's at eight?"

I told him about the meeting.

"Can I come?"

"I would think certainly not. This is a meeting about you, not for you. But, sure, come along. Let Field kick you out."

I did what I promised. When we returned to the college I found Partridge, the nearest neighbour among the part-timers, in his office and Ginger in ours. I took ten minutes with Partridge, embellishing my role of leaky vessel by saying that I had heard that the administration was interested in Richard's idea and we ought to be prepared. To Ginger, I just said that he ought to come; this could be a historic meeting.

chapter thirty-five

I was still leaving the question of what to do with the papers until I had a chance to think through who properly owned them. The connection between the Garrick and the Selby was pretty murky. Probably the story of a workman stashing behind the mirror of a room in the Garrick what he had come across in the Selby made as much sense as anything, except that it was unlikely that a workman, a carpenter, say, would have immediately identified the papers as valuable, I thought, in my elitist academic way. Yes, it was, the private eye said, because the story was legendary and there is nothing that carpenters like more than legends about the places they are renovating, except, perhaps, ghost stories.

Thus it was very likely the carpenter had been told the story of the famous guest, come across the papers, and put them in his tool chest. Then, feeling the possibility that the goods were warmer than he had realized, and hoping now just for a reward, he had "found" them on his next job, the Garrick, and turned them over to the owner. Now the carpenter was dead, and there was no one to get any other truth from, so the trail to establish the ownership must start with some papers found at the Garrick, left behind by a tenant escaping his bill. Something like that.

Then there was the original bookseller, Curry. Looking in the history of the papers for an honest man, I still chose Curry, who, approached by the owner of the Garrick, agreed to find out what the papers were worth and had them stolen off him before he could do it. The Garrick owner responded to the news of the theft by assuming that Curry was a crook like so many of the people he knew and threatened to thump him, but never recovered the papers.

Curry paid the Garrick owner a thousand dollars, to keep the man away. He was afraid that the hotel keeper might reappear one day with some friends to search his bookshop, or burn it down. The Garrick man was smart, though. He kept his temper, but retained some kind of claim on the papers should they ever appear. Now Curry was dead, and Mrs. Curry had a receipt for the thousand her husband had paid the Garrick owner, and the hotel keeper had hung on to his claim.

Then Tyler came along and bought the bookstore. Had he therefore bought Curry's rights to the ownership of the papers if they were found? He says so. Mrs. Curry doesn't agree. So when Tyler discovered the papers, he "robbed" himself. He saw enough validity in the claims of Gresham and Mrs. Curry that he didn't want to dispute them, so he planned to sell the papers quietly. There was something wrong with this, but it was the best I could do for the moment.

All this I had put together after consulting my bibliophile colleague with some "What if?" questions, when I began to wonder about the original theft.

"Are you talking about those papers again?" Tensor asked with affected weariness.

"Yes," I said. "I think that maybe they were never stolen in the first place, and I'm wondering how easy it would have been for Curry to have faked a robbery and disposed of them privately."

"Against that you have to put Curry's reputation as an absolutely honest dealer. If he was brought a genuinely rare and valuable book, he'd make a fair offer, either to buy it, or to sell it on the person's behalf."

"On consignment, you mean?"

"No, on commission. Acting as an agent, everything done in the open. You know that Tyler is moving down to Front Street?"

"When is it supposed to happen?"

"Any day, or any week. I imagine moving that many books is more than an afternoon's work. Someone said he's closed already. I understand that the building has been sold to a salvage expert. Apparently everything is valuable—the wide pine floorboards, the wall panelling, the very bricks. There are even a couple of antique cast iron fireplaces."

"Which may be where Tyler found the papers. In some hiding place of Curry's. But you say Curry was no crook."

"He was known as an honest man."

"We'll never know now, will we?"

And that was that, but not for long. In my book, the papers still belonged to Mrs. Curry.

The meeting of the sessionals took place the next morning in Room 402, a lecture theatre fitted out for science courses with a bench with a sink and taps in place of the usual lectern.

The room held a hundred and forty students and I thought it was badly chosen as a place for our eight or ten sessionals to meet, but when I arrived, a few minutes before the hour, the place was full, and one or two members of the faculty were sitting on the stairs between the tiered sections. It looked as if every sessional teacher in the college had come to listen.

Richard Costril was there; as was Fred, our chairman.

Nothing happened for a few minutes while we waited to learn whose meeting this was, in procedural terms, then Field took charge and invited Fred to speak.

Fred began by questioning the presence of the hundred-odd people from outside the department. He was told by a sessional instructor from the Geography department not to act the innocent, please, that of course the meeting was of interest to others, that is, might affect others, or could one day, so let's get on with it without a lot of farting around.

He was quite rude, an outsider might have thought, but he had been a sessional for twelve years and was secure in his seniority, and very pissed off. I experienced then, for the first time, the truism that a lot of managing takes place with the consent of the managed, and its success depends on the personal relationships of the manager with his managed. Fred was our chairman and we liked him, so we granted him the privilege of managing us. The Geography sessional, however, felt no loyalty towards him, and you could feel the guy-ropes creaking as the winds of democracy and anarchy (in the true, non-violent sense) blew on the administration's house.

Fred nodded, wisely treating the interruption as rhetorical, then continued, "If you don't mind, though, I came to say a word to my department about an internal situation that has developed, and when I've said my piece, I'll answer any questions from them as best I can, but not from anyone outside the department. I think you need a dean for that. Okay?"

"Not okay," the geographer said immediately. "You are a member of the administration and therefore ..."

Field held up his hand. "One thing at a time, Cyril. This *is* a meeting of the English part-timers. It seems right that you should hold a watching brief, so by all means stay, but don't participate any further." He didn't even glance around to seek the tacit approval of the department.

The geographer said, or started to say, "But ..." and one of the sessionals in the Philosophy department leaned over and said, "Cyril, shut the fuck up," and the room grunted its assent in various ways, and the meeting began.

"The idea," Fred said, "of giving sessional and other non-tenured people a voice in the appointment of a new chairman has reached the ears of the president and the chairman of the Board, and they have asked me through the dean to let you know informally that they are interested, just in the principle, of course. As you know the election is on Tuesday and there is not a lot of time to think it through between now and then. But the Board committee on faculty affairs is meeting today to look at the idea. Remember it is only a temporary appointment and a good time to try out a new idea without committing the whole college to a change of policy."

Cyril said, before he could be squashed, "Aren't you just putting it off so that it will go away?"

Fred said, "I believe I've said my piece. I'll only add, informally, that I have heard that the chairman thinks the idea has merit." He stepped off the dais.

"Christ" I said to Ginger. "Again. That means they're really going to do it. We have to meet."

"We *are* meeting, aren't we?"

"Just the department sessionals." I called Field over and told him to finish the meeting while there was still time for the English department to meet.

chapter thirty-six

Field had never made much impression on me. He's doing a thesis on the influence of Ezra Pound on Marshall McLuhan or the other way round, so I know he's clever, but he seems to have no competitive instinct, none of the desire to shine that the seminars in graduate school train you up in, and I assumed that he had retreated from the arena when he found he had no taste for that particular fray. In my experience, such students usually switch to Anglo-Saxon or linguistics, where trickiness of interpretation isn't expected of them. Or they drop out altogether and get jobs in the private schools. But Field has continued to accumulate the material and arguments he will need to finish his thesis.

We all liked him without rating him highly enough. Now, and in the days that followed, he showed his true worth—or perhaps just his other side—a man with a field marshal's baton in his book bag. He listened to me now, nodded at the end, said "Right," and stood up to speak. In doing so, he seemed to me to be throwing off his disguise. Even his voice, which I always thought of as cosy, cracked out and bounced off the back windows of the room. It was only his teaching voice, of course, but I'd never heard it before. (The tenured faculty is continually assessing the sessionals, but we, the sessionals, don't get to see each other teach.)

"Can I have your attention," he said, and got it immediately. "We have only half an hour left, and with the election imminent some important things to consider. We will be happy to join with you all again next week but right now the English sessionals have to meet to deal with our problem." He stopped, nodded, and stared around the room at the non-English sessionals, who took his point and left. "And you, please, Richard," Field said, forestalling me as I realized that Richard was making himself at home, ready to join the new meeting of English sessionals.

"But it was my idea," Richard said.

"And we are all deeply grateful to you. But right now we have to consider how we are going to respond if your idea continues to have merit in the eyes of our masters. So, please, we're running short of time."

Richard rose, protesting still. "I think of myself as an honorary member of this group by dint of ..."

"And so do we, Richard, but we remember you have other loyalties now, too, both personal and collegial, so without further discussion, unless the group overrules me, I ask you to go."

Nobody spoke. I pretended to be engrossed with a question from a colleague who was seated behind me, and by the time I turned round, Richard was gone.

Field said, by way of making us feel better about Richard, "First of all, we can't really speak openly with one of them in the room, as Richard used to know. If we do get the vote, he wants it, and in fairness he should only have the same forum as the others, which is what I am about to propose.

"Now I don't know what the hell is happening here but there seem to be rumours of a tiny crack in the administration's dike. The president has apparently been overheard to speak with interest about the idea of giving us each a portion of a vote so that we may no longer claim to be disenfranchised, and that is how I suggest we regard it. Already—"he looked at his watch—"they won't be able to go back on this without increasing our hostility. I think we should act in an 'as if' fashion; that is, we should assume there will be an election that we will participate in. But we must remember that we have special interests, and also that we have not been privy to the campaign rhetoric so far. We are ignorant of their platforms and we need to cut some planks of our own. Therefore I propose we have an election meeting here at the same time on Monday morning and let the candidates pitch us. We haven't time to do a subtle analysis of the possible results of the vote, and there certainly isn't time for a poll, or anything like that, just as the candidates don't have time to canvass us individually. So let's give them one short try at winning our hearts and minds on Monday. All in favour?"

I think everyone felt as I did, that it was a bit of a lark, an opportunity to do a bit of shit-disturbing as a group, so, instead of the endless "But, Mr. Speaker ..." stuff you usually get at academic meetings, a ragged, but unopposed "Aye" rang out like a cheer as the bell sounded for the nine o'clock class.

As they filed out, Field stopped me to ask a question. "Don't we need to let the administration know what's up?" he asked.

"Why? Let them be surprised."

"Right. If they find out just ahead of time, without a lot of warning, they may be bustled into doing something silly." He was going from strength to strength.

"I'll have a chat with Fred," I said. "He's still chairman until the election, and he seems to have the ear of the Kremlin."

Fred was waiting for me. His is a corner office and if he leaves the door open he has a narrow view out to the hall. I could have avoided his eye by going the long way round the floor, but as I got off the elevator I had half a mind to walk in on him. So I was ready when he called out, in jocular fashion, "What's up, Joe?" as if we had just met on the street corner.

I was tempted to tease him by staying just out of reach in the corridor and shouting back, "Nothing much, Dick. How about you?" but I refrained. I paused, nodded, and responded to his wig-wagging hand by going in and sitting down.

"How'd the secret meeting go?" he asked. "Planning a sit-in of this office, are you?" He laughed, pretending to joke. "You want to close the door?"

I got up and closed the door without quite shutting it, thus intimating that I had nothing secret to discuss, just trying to keep out the noise. "It was just a private meeting, Fred. We didn't have much time and we didn't want a bunch of outsiders and voyeurs using up valuable minutes."

"Uh-huh. So what did you talk about?"

"There wasn't any discussion to speak of, if you know what I mean. We learned that the administration was very sympathetic to our need to participate in the election, and we wanted to sort out and collectivize our response."

"Where did you hear that we are ... they are sympathetic?"

"It's all over the college, Fred. You heard it everywhere today." His lying in wait for me like this, calling me in to "chat" was the best news we'd had so far. It meant that Field was right: the administration took us far more seriously than we were taking ourselves.

I believe that at this point, if asked, all the sessionals would have said we were just stirring it up, not really hoping for much. But Fred was making it clear we shouldn't underestimate ourselves. We had them worried.

I guessed that until now the administration had planned to seem interested in the election, would perhaps next year set up a small committee to study it. Given this latest turn of events, I thought I should water the seeds of unease.

"There were a dozen people there, Fred, and every single one of them had heard it from a different source. One of them said he heard it from the President's assistant in the washroom. Not the assistant who hangs out in the washroom—the guy said he heard it in the washroom from the President's assistant." I smiled. "Misplaced modifier," I said.

"Who was that?"

"I forget. Another one heard it from Jack Boudreau, the P.R. flack."

"How would that asshole know?"

"That's what I said. Another one got it from a student reporter on the *Hambletonian*. Incredible, isn't it? Yesterday no one had heard of it."

"What do you make of it?"

"Nothing yet. But one of the new guys—I can't tell you his name of, course, Dick, he doesn't have much seniority—he said he thought you, the administration, were flying a windsock, testing the waters."

"I don't think you test waters with a windsock. Never mind. He thinks the rumour came from the top?"

"Most of them do. I mean most of the part-timers think that."

"That's ridiculous."

"Well, there you are. The only hard news is that the pressure of time is making us have an election meeting tomorrow morning at eight o'clock. We want to know what the candidates can do for us, the sessionals."

"Can I come?"

"If it were up to me ... no, of course you can come. The question is whether you will be allowed to stay. I would think not. Some of the sessionals are quite bitter about their treatment over the years and they might speak a bit freely, so I would think we would move a closed session."

"So much for free and open debate, eh, when you guys get into power." He tried to sneer, but he was alarmed and I could see he would hustle off to tell the dean as soon as I left.

"Fred," I said. "*Fred*. Think. Two of the sessionals only came this year. You can kick them out at Christmas, and I think you could probably cut a few corners in the timetables and get rid of two more by the spring. Do you really expect them to speak out with you around?"

"*You* feel pretty secure, do you?"

"Yes, I do. Shouldn't I?" Saying it coldly, very still.

He hurried to wash off any trace of threat. "I hope so, Joe. You're one of the best teachers we have."

"If you don't have tenure, you have to be good, don't you?"

chapter thirty-seven

On Friday the news of the break-in at Tyler's store was on television with a picture of the broken door, and on Saturday the newspapers published the whole story, along with a full account of the Hemingway Papers, and the story of the early robbery.

Tyler, I learned later, spent the weekend looking for his own thief and by Tuesday he had narrowed the suspects down to me. I found out how later.

When I returned to the office from my *Henry IV* class I found a message on my desk from Masaka saying someone had called to say he would wait for me outside the office at five when I came back from my last class.

This put me in a slightly delicate position because I had rearranged my schedule to get rid of that class and give me a free afternoon to work on my novel. In principle, this was acceptable to the authorities if it could be done without upsetting the students too much, but you were supposed to request the change through the chairman. By making my own arrangements and letting Fred know after the fact I was slightly abusing my seniority. Technically I had cancelled a class without permission, but the only problem that might have arisen would have been if the dean happened to come looking for me. Now, someone, some student probably, looking for an extension on his essay, had checked my timetable and claimed an audience when I was scheduled to be on campus.

On another day I would have waited, spent the time marking assignments, but today I knew I wouldn't be able to keep my mind off Hemingway. So I decided not to get the message, not to go back to my office, and took the basement route to the parking lot to avoid the student traffic between classes.

At three-thirty I put the key in my front door, and tried to turn it. The lock was jammed, but while I was pressing this way and that the door began to open. Puzzled—no more than that yet—I pushed a little and the door yielded, and finally I pushed out of the way whatever was behind the door—an armchair, it turned out—and squeezed through the gap into the hall. I wondered what Carole was up to that involved moving furniture about.

Then the puzzlement became tinged with doubt, creating the level of goosiness you can feel in broad daylight when you hear a well-read ghost story. As I tried to make sense of what I was seeing, the doubt turned into solid fear, not yet terror, but the feeling that there was something loose in the apartment.

The mess began with the hall closet: all the coats had been thrown out into the hall and the shelves above emptied, the gloves and scarves dumped onto the floor. I heard someone slam the door of the bathroom closet, and a familiar character emerged from the bathroom; familiar, but in my panic I couldn't immediately identify him. Then Tyler appeared from the bedroom and I simultaneously identified the bathroom intruder as Brian, his bookstore assistant.

The phone rang. "Leave it alone," Tyler said. "Now, where are those papers?"

I could see that they had gone through the apartment, unsystematically tumbling everything on to the floor or the beds. The bookshelves had been cleared; the closets and desk drawers had been emptied out, turned upside down, raked over. The pack of paper obscuring the whereabouts of the Hemingway Papers had been thrown aside, presumably to see if something was hidden under it, but the pack itself lay apparently intact under Carole's desk in a mess of loose sheets of paper.

"What makes you think I've got them?" I asked. Then, a bit late, "What papers?"

"You had them on Thursday night."

I found an ounce of courage. "So call the police."

"I want the papers first. Then I might."

"We both want them," Brian said, apparently to double the threat. I wondered what Tyler had told him to get him to come along. Brian wasn't a thug, and Tyler must have conned him into believing that his boss had been victimised in some way. His lack of impressiveness gave me a bit more courage.

"Call the police," I said. "Tell them what you've done here. Tell them about stealing your own books. Tell them about the papers."

Tyler said, "Maybe I will. See, Brian and I dropped by this afternoon to ask you to return the papers you stole from my car the other night, and say no more about it." He was explaining how he would put it in the future, rehearsing his lines. "You lost your head, is all, at the idea of getting your hands on this rare manuscript. Your moral sense has become bent as the result of spying on me this last two or three weeks. I'd say you're in for theft, maybe more."

"Wouldn't the insurance company have something to say about you stealing your own books?"

"Who says I stole them? You? Word of a thief trying to get away with his own larceny?"

"A common thief," Brian said.

I said, "How come you didn't announce you'd found the papers?"

"He did," Brian said. "He told me."

"See?" Tyler said. "We've got a stand-off."

"No," I said. "You robbed your own store. I saw you."

Tyler stared at me. This was the one thing that had happened, the one he couldn't get around. Brian looked puzzled.

Then Tyler's face cleared. "Bluff," he said. "Good, but bluff. See, you may think I robbed my store, but you didn't see it, because you were parked on Harbord Street while the store was robbed, collecting the evidence of my affair. You saw me arrive, and you saw me and the lady leave. How could you have seen me robbing my store? I was having an affair, and you were watching me."

"I saw you leave twice. The first time I followed you to your store, which you robbed. I have a picture of that. Then you came back to your room on Harbord. I saw you put the books and briefcase in the car. I have a picture of that, too."

"And you took the stuff from my car. Right?"

"You don't have a witness to say I took anything from your car."

"I could find one."

"Me," Brian said.

King Tyler had acquired a Fool, and it was irritating. "Tell you what," I said to Brian. "Why don't you watch out the window for parking officials so I can talk to your boss." I turned back to Tyler. "If we get that far I might have to explain to the insurance company why I have pictures of you having an affair with your own wife the night when her sister or cousin was sick. That was a good trick, but it didn't work. The pictures are very clear. I might even get to finish my last report, the one that will have the condom packet stapled to it. I imagine your wife won't mind that you really were screwing her sister, not just manufacturing evidence, will she? I mean if I could help you to prove you really were having an affair then this story of mine will sound like I'm making it up, won't it?"

And so the end game had begun, the game of trying to find out what the other man didn't want to happen, and threatening him with it. I thought I had a lot on Tyler, but he had already showed me how he might take it apart.

I said, "And I still have the papers," and tried to stroll nonchalantly past Tyler into the living room. It was stupid.

He hit me hard, on the side of my face, so that I sailed across the room, landing, with my head bent into my neck, up against the bookcase.

chapter thirty-eight

I've read enough noir fiction and seen enough celluloid saloon fights in black and white *and* colour to believe I knew what hitting people was like, but this was real. I realized later that I had only ever imagined myself as the hitter, never the hit. When it seems likely that the pretty male lead is going to have his hands smashed with the butt of a gun, I have always dug deep into my popcorn, planning to look up when they stop screaming. In fact, I know nothing about being hit; those times that Bronson's fist travelled *towards* the camera had never fooled me. I knew that the screen would go black before he hurt himself. Now, it felt as if I had been smashed across the face with a piece of two-by-four.

I shook my head, remembering from the countless brawls I'd seen that that was how you cleared it. I heard Tyler's voice coming through the fog.

"The thing is," he was saying, "You've been reading too many books. You think you can cook up a cute story and get everyone to believe you, like now, when you're thinking of telling the cops we beat you up. You want to know where I've been all afternoon? At the racetrack. A dozen witnesses will say so, and you'll look like you're trying to frame me. How about you?" he asked Brian. "Where've you been?"

"I'll think of something," Brian said. "In the shop, with the door locked, packing books for the move."

"There," Tyler said to me. "See? Now where are these papers?"

"On their way to New York."

Tyler's face filled with blood and grew shiny.

Brian said, "What does he mean?"

"He means he's sent them to a dealer down there. Right?"

"You've got it," I agreed. The longer we talked the better I felt. My only weapon, words, seemed to be having an effect.

"Hey," I said suddenly. "There's someone missing: the dwarf."

"What are you talking about?"

"The dwarf. You have to have a dwarf. See, guys like you travel in threes. There's the boss, that's you; then there's the jester, that's Brian here, though he's more of a Fool. No, no, not an idiot, Brian. The Fool is the brightest one in the play. So, the boss, the jester, and the dwarf. Always a trio and a dwarf: Stephano, Trinculo, and Caliban. Check it out: there's *always* a dwarf. Probably goes back to the old Roman comedies."

"What the fuck are you talking about?"

I wasn't sure myself, but it held things up for a while. Then he made a made a show of elaborately arranging his hitting arm, shifting his shoulder muscles, clubbing his fist. Hearing nothing from me, he took a step towards me.

"Fook off owa that," a voice said, as nearly as I can represent it, and a shape burst through the door into the room, bore down on Tyler and swung its head in a short arc, smashing Tyler in the forehead with its own.

Tyler went soft, and the shape hit him again, but this time with a fist that disappeared up to the wrist beneath Tyler's sternum.

Tyler sat on the floor, making long *er-er-er-er* noises. The shape turned to Brian, who was making signs of wanting to interfere, and landed an orange boot in his crotch, causing him to collapse next to Tyler.

The shape said to me. "If you can run, let's get awa out of this." He pointed to Tyler. "I had surprise on my side, you might say, but this bugger'll come round soon enough."

It was Ginger. He was right. When the element of surprise ran out, we might be less than a match for them. Tyler was giving off waves of aggression even as he fought for breath, and for all we knew would soon reach for a gun or a knife or a cosh. Brian stood now with his back to the wall, looking at me with hate.

If I'd had my wits about me I would have realized that we could have drawn them away and returned for the papers later, but all my instincts told me not to leave them to be discovered, so I grabbed the pack of paper from Carole's desk and ran after Ginger, who was already at the door. Tyler didn't miss the significance of this and gave a kind of moan as we disappeared, and staggered after us right away with Brian hobbling in pursuit.

"Across the street," I shouted to Ginger. "Next right."

We pounded along, with Tyler and Brian behind us, getting fitter all the time, not gaining but not losing, either. I put on a burst to get in front of Ginger and led him down the alley, and then I was unlocking the car. I thought we'd lost them but when we turned on to Dupont, the yellow Volvo appeared in my rear-view mirror.

Visions of Steve McQueen in *Bullitt* danced in my head, but Toronto rises quite gently from the lake without any significant humps to punch the Toyota van into the air. Besides, it was the beginning of the rush hour and every road had steady traffic in every lane. So instead of *Bullitt* we played the car game where you can see someone you dislike two cars behind who has already cut off a couple of other cars and you decide not to let the bastard in when he gets to you, and you both deke in and out of the one-car gaps, looking to slip into the first hole that appears.

I took us across Macpherson, went south on Yonge, and turned left on Davenport to Bloor. There I travelled two blocks, dawdling slightly with Tyler three cars behind me, then, (my first touch of *Bullitt*) there being a gap, I dived left down the ramp on to Mount Pleasant Boulevard, cut slightly dangerously into the centre lane and back to the kerb lane, and said to Ginger, "I think we've lost them."

"Like fuck," Ginger said, and there they were again, parallel to us as we screamed up Mount Pleasant towards St. Clair.

I accelerated slightly, tailgated a cement truck, braked sharply, then took a right along Moore Avenue as they went too far to follow me. I carried on over to Bayview and turned south. I know this part of the city well from having cycled through it on my way to the tennis club. "A piece of cake," I said. "*Un morceau de gateau.*"

"Aye," Ginger said. "So it is for those two coonts." He gestured in the mirror at the Volvo coming up fast.

How the hell did they get there?

I switched to the centre lane and caught the light at Pottery Road and then really did a little McQueen-type driving out to Broadview. This time I didn't relax. I drove straight south to Queen, then turned to pick up Richmond and headed across the city. Finally, there was no sign of the Volvo.

"They got caught at the light," Ginger said.

"Now, I've got an idea. Those guys want me and these." I held up the papers. "So home isn't safe for me at the moment; I'm going to hide out for a bit." I reached into the glove compartment and brought out the cellular phone. "Carole knows this number. Tell her I'll call as soon as I see what's happening. You go on back to the apartment and park outside. They'll find you."

"Aye, and that guy will pound the shit out of me."

"No. Tell him exactly what we've done. Tell him you dropped me at Richmond and Bathurst, and I gave you instructions to find them and say so. Now I'll phone my boss ... no, maybe later."

"You know what you're doing?"

"I'm not sure. I think so. I need time to think. What did you want, by the way?"

"How do you mean?"

"Lucky for me you came by the apartment. What did you want?"

"I just thought you might like a beer."

"Some other time?"

"Sure."

chapter thirty-nine

I found a cab to take me up Spadina to Harbord, and dived down the alley behind Glinka's building. I was counting on Glinka being home and on his general goodwill after that.

He answered my ring and let me into the hall.

"I want the room," I said. "Is it still vacant?"

"Sure. How long?"

"Just for a few days."

"Minimum is a week. A hundred fifty dollars."

"Can we start with four days? A hundred?"

"How can you tell? What it is, you get writer's block, you might be here all winter."

I had almost forgotten my cover. "No, no," I said, laughingly. "Just some revisions. My wife's having the apartment repainted. I can't work there. Five days?"

"A week. Tomorrow is end of month. I could lose a month's rent to do you a favour."

I looked in my wallet. So did Glinka. "A down payment?" I asked. "Forty?"

"Fifty. I'll hold it until six o'clock for the rest."

"Two *hours*?"

He pointed at my VISA card. "There's a bank machine on the corner."

I gave him fifty and took the key. "No luggage?" he asked. "No bag? Nothing? You just looking for somewhere to bring a girlfriend like the last guy. He give you the idea."

"No way. I've got ten pages to write and I'm done. I'll go home tonight and get a toothbrush and stuff."

"And a hundred dollars."

I let myself in the room and sat down on the cot to think. First I wondered how Tyler had gotten on to me so fast. I wondered if Glinka had shopped me. He was jolly enough with me, but I had no idea what his response would have been if Tyler had asked him if he had seen any suspicious characters around. It would have been tempting to chat about me.

I crossed the room to look down on Harbord Street, then jumped back as I put myself in full view of the sausage vendor and realized at the same time how it must have been.

Tyler had quit his love nest once he had performed behind the blind so I could testify I had seen him. By then my job was done and he could assume that I had gone home. Then, possibly without even checking his car, he had driven home, and been called back to the store by the police. When he finally went to put the papers in a safe place, he found them gone and he knew he had to start looking for a thief near his pad.

So he had played the investigator, asking around if anyone had seen a suspicious character near his car. Of course he had to have asked the sausage vendor who had just about every parked car in his sights, and knew every character on the street. The sausage man would have responded to the question with eager enmity.

Sure he'd seen the prick near Tyler's car, the one who used to sit there every Tuesday and Thursday night keeping tabs on his wife who was shacked up

*with someone in that room up there, getting what
the creep couldn't give her, probably. Sure, and
another thing, this Tuesday he took off for most of
the night. But he came back and stayed a while,
then he was gone within the half-hour. Could he
identify him? Sure he could. Prick-face.*

So the next day Tyler considered his options.
Everybody, including me now, was operating on both sides
of the law and Tyler's main concern was to get the papers
back. He wanted the books, too, of course, because he had
to stay with this story about having been broken into until
he found out what I was up to.

At that point, he knew I had the papers, but he needed
to know if I was a bit of a thief, maybe, crooked enough
to try to sell them. He knew I probably would have no idea
of how to go about fencing them, which was also a problem because he had to fear that, stumbling around, asking,
"Who wants my papers?" I would cause his whole caper
to be exposed.

So when I came home, Tyler and Brian had been doing
the first search of my apartment, just in case I hadn't
already rented a locker or a safety-deposit box while I
decided what to do.

All this seemed clear.

chapter forty

But I still didn't know what to do except stay out of the way of Tyler, and so I thought renting his old love nest for a few days was clever and ironic, but with the sausage vendor parked across the street, it was turning out to be stupid.

I had to assume he was now a willing watchdog for Tyler, one who had the advantage (for Tyler) of knowing by sight whom to watch for. Tyler was anxious, because every hour contained the possibility that I might go to the cops if I hadn't done so already. At one point I did think that was the best thing for me to do, but another turn of the wheel showed me that he still might be able to deny my whole story, and he wouldn't rest until he had made his point with me. That he would be responsible for my being found in a back alley, needing crutches, would be utterly unprovable, but there I'd be. And Tyler might get the papers.

I called home on my cell-phone and Carole was there. I told her the story and she said she was going to call the police. I told her I wasn't ready to do that yet and she said she was, and where was I now?

I demurred, and she said to someone else in the room, "Where did you leave him?"

I said, "Is Ginger there? Let me speak to him."

Ginger said, "Go to the police, you stupid fooker."

I said, "Not yet. But I'm a bit concerned about Carole. This may take a couple of days. Can you stay there with her?"

"Of course," he said, his BBC Northern accent returning. "I'll tell Carole."

I heard him talking quietly to Carole and her quiet shriek of "For God's sake," and then, to me, "If I need Ginger to stay here, then you should go to the police."

"Not yet," I said. "Look out the window. You see a yellow Volvo?"

"Ginger's watching it now. They're sitting right outside."

"They're waiting for me to come home."

"Go to the police."

"Not yet. Stay there with Ginger. Let me talk to him again."

"Shit," she said. "Here he is now."

"This is me again. What's up?"

"Ginger, don't leave the apartment," I said "The thing is, I want to get these guys to do something stupid."

"Why?"

"It's a long story, but ideally those guys should be in jail and Mrs. Curry should have the papers."

"But I thought they all …"

"For Christ's sake, Ginger. I can't go through it now. It's just that I see a chance for this all to come out right."

"I'll look after Carole for you."

"Thanks, mate."

I looked at the sausage vendor across the street. If I wanted to show myself on Dundas, I would have to get a disguise of some kind, even just to go to the machine on the corner to get Glinka his money, and to pick up a coffee and sandwich to go, and a toothbrush.

First, I had to do something with the papers.

The room didn't offer much in the way of hiding places that would fool Tyler. It was just a space about sixteen foot square with a door on one side and a window on the other. There was a table, a chair, and the cot, and nothing else, not even a closet. Along one wall Glinka had installed a piece of one-inch pipe from which hung three battered wire coat-hangers. An advertisement for a Chinese take-out was taped to the back of the door under a coat-hook. That was it.

I thought I might have to carry the papers around with me until I looked up and saw what Glinka had done to the ceiling. A false ceiling of foam plastic sheets a quarter-inch thick was suspended in a thin metal frame. I started to move the table under the right place then remembered to pull down the blind before I climbed up. When I stood on the table and pushed against the ceiling one of the plastic sheets lifted easily. I wiggled it out so I could see into the space between the ceiling and the roof. I had to put the chair on the table to get high enough, and the chair was on castors and had a swivel seat. (I've been tipped on the floor by this type of chair just by leaning forward.) I took off my shoes and put them on two legs of the chair. I wrapped my sock around the threaded shaft that allowed the chair to swivel and screwed it down tight. I was pleased to feel when I climbed up that it felt cemented in place.

I pushed my head and shoulders up into the hole; as I suspected, the false ceiling was purely cosmetic, the kind of thing you put up in a basement to cover up the crappy-looking joists and pipes. Moving carefully, I took the papers up to lay them on the metal framing, but it seemed too flimsy, and I found a place where a pipe turned through a right-angle and formed enough of a platform to rest the papers on. As I climbed down, there was a distinct wobble from the chair and I was glad to get my bare foot on the desk.

chapter forty-one

I left the building and turned back down the alley to Richmond Street where I found a bank machine and extracted Glinka's money.

Next I found a barber, one who still called himself a barber and not a stylist, in a three-chair shop down a side street. None of the chairs were occupied, and the five old men who were sitting around the walls were just hanging out.

They stopped talking when I walked in, wondering what I wanted. The sole barber, a man in his seventies at least, gave one of the chairs a vicious slap with the cloth he carried on his shoulder, and I sat down. He wrapped the cloth around my neck and wiped his hand on my hair. The whole scene reminded me of Ring Lardner's story.

"Trim?" the barber asked.

"Take it all off."

The hangers-on perked up and focused on me. "He wants it all off," one of them said to his neighbour.

"Take it all off?" the barber asked.

"That's right. All of it." It was my first thought when I decided to hide. My hair is black and thick, and as a teenager I used to have to glue it to keep it down. I needed to reshape it.

"Shave it?"

"No!" Jesus. I had no idea what my naked head would look like. Pitted? Discoloured? Even smooth and shiny I didn't want it. I've always felt sorry for people who have suffered a total loss of hair from shock or creeping alopecia, but all naked heads look obscene to me and the idea of choosing to have one just wasn't on.

"I thought you was a bit old for it. Mostly punks, ain't they? Kids?"

"Some of them are older," one of the spectators said.

"*Old* skinheads look fucking ridiculous," said another.

"So what'll it be?" the barber asked.

I held my thumb and finger a quarter of an inch apart, keeping my hand to one side so the kibitzers couldn't see.

"You sure?"

I held out my hand, the thumb and finger still apart, and moved it back and forth to confirm that I knew what I was asking. The spectators at the end of the row craned to read the gesture.

"Right," Sweeney said, and started to snip. He worked for about fifteen minutes, then held up a mirror to show me the back of my head. "How's that?"

I thought at first that it was someone else. It took years off me.

"Perfect," I said.

One of the spectators said, "You should dye it yellow. Like blond. Even the Chinese kids round here are doing it. But you might look like a queer."

I paid the barber. Then I thought of a way of shutting this gang up. "I'm in a play," I said. "I'm a Russian student in a play. I'm just getting the character right. Is there a second-hand clothes store around here?"

The leading kibitzer said, "That's all there is around here. Try Fab Gear across the street. "What do you need?"

"An overcoat," I said.

"Goodwill," one said. The others nodded.

"You need glasses," one of them said. "For being a student, like."

He was right; it was the flaw in my costume. "I need a pair of granny glasses," I said. "The kind I can look over the top of. Where can I get a pair round here? You know the kind I mean? The ones with wire rims that old professors used to wear in Hollywood."

"Gimme twenty bucks."

"How do you know what they cost?"

"They all cost twenty bucks ..."

"Can I trust him?" I asked the others, jocularly.

"He brings back the change when we send him for coffee."

I gave the man a twenty and he was back in five minutes with exactly what I wanted. I put them on too high at first and when I looked through them the room swirled around until I pulled them down to the end of my nose. I looked in the mirror. Pure Trigorin.

I took a streetcar across to Jarvis, to the Goodwill charity shop and found what I wanted immediately, an overcoat of a size that a clown would use to conceal his stilts. I slipped it on.

"I *told* you it was too big," the volunteer worker said. "It's dragging."

"So it is." I kicked the skirt to one side the way I'd seen grand dames in movies coming down staircases do, and stepped forward to see if it tripped me up. If I shrugged my shoulders, it was just right.

"Isn't it going to be kind of warm?" The worker asked. "You look a little goofy."

Just the look I was after. "How much?" I asked.

"Five dollars."

I paid him and left the store to walk along the street. I checked myself in a couple of store windows and felt so secure that I actually hoped a yellow Volvo would come curb-crawling by, but I stayed unmolested all the way back to my room.

Not knowing how long I was going to be holed up, I bought a coffee and a chicken salad sandwich on the way, a couple of Kit-Kat bars and a second-hand paperback, an old Elmore Leonard I had read long enough ago to be worth revisiting, and went back to the room.

I called Carole when I was settled in. I said, "I can't tell you where I am. Everything all right? Ginger there?"

She said, "Everything is not all right. Unless I hear from you why not, I'm calling the police first thing in the morning. What kind of game are you playing?"

"It's not a game, Carole. Didn't Ginger tell you? I've been clobbered once. Is he there?"

"No, he's not. I'm not there, either. Ginger brought me here."

"Where is here?" I asked, like a literary critic.

"*Here* is with Arlette."

"Their place? Berky and Arlette?"

"Of course. Ginger went home after he'd brought me here."

"Christ, that means they will know where you are."

"Not the way Ginger drove. We went from the Annex to Upper Canada College via the Lakeshore, if you can believe it. Ginger said he's never driven in Canada before, on the wrong side of the road, like. I can tell you we weren't followed." She was very angry.

I took shelter in my role. "I don't want to speak longer than I have to. Don't call the police. I'll call you by nine in the morning. Don't leave Arlette's until I call you."

"Why? This is a cell phone."

"Oh, right. So I'll call you." I disconnected.

chapter forty-two

The next morning I put on my costume and went out for breakfast. I called Fred at the college to tell him how sick I was and to cancel my classes for the day, at least. I had no idea how long I was going to rest in my current mode, but I needed some kind of cooling-off period before I met up with Tyler and Brian again.

I also called my boss at the agency. I had let him know something of what I thought Tyler was up to, what we were really being paid by his wife for, and all that had now been confirmed. Obviously as a good citizen, there was no way I was going to let Tyler get away with the book scam, but dealing with the papers would take more thought. I was sure now that the reason Tyler had not announced the discovery of the papers in the first place was that he had no intention of dealing Gresham or Mrs. Curry in, so now the minimum restitution of justice would be to let Mrs. Curry and Gresham know what was going on and let them take it from there.

This time my boss went crazy. He made me go through the whole story twice until he understood it, then said, "I'm calling Donker. The fraud squad. He reads a lot; he'll know what to do. I'll have him take this off our hands.

Where are the books?" I said, "They're safe. Never mind them. It's these papers. I want to be sure Gresham and Mrs. Curry stake their claim, especially Mrs. Curry."

"Never mind Mrs. Curry," he shouted. "She's probably the goddam ringleader. Get down here and bring those books and papers with you and be ready to hand them over to Donker."

"I'll hand them over once Tyler has agreed to give Mrs. Curry and Gresham their share."

He said, "Let them sort that out when they get out of jail."

I said, "No."

He shouted at me, a lot of stuff about obstructing the police, but I hung on for another ten minutes, and won, temporarily. I just didn't trust Tyler not to make the papers disappear again, once he had his hands on them, or swindle her in some other way.

"All right," Atkinson said, finally. "A meeting here, in the office, with Donker in the back room."

"Why?"

"To arrest Tyler, of course. He's perpetrated a fraud, don't you understand? Pretending to have stuff stolen. The insurance company isn't going to smile at that."

"They can't prove it without the books,"

"You *bring* the books."

"No."

"Then the agency is having nothing to do with this. You do what you like. I'm going to call Donker, and when you come out of jail where you'll be for failing to co-operate with the police, I'll fire you."

"Try this," I pleaded. "Forget this whole conversation. I'll hang up. When I call you back, I'll ask you to make a room free for me for a meeting with our client on the Tyler infidelity case. That's all I'll tell you, then there won't be any collusion on your part."

"Why, for Christ's sake? Why? Why? Why?"

"I told you, for Mrs. Curry's sake, and because I know the whole story."

I disconnected and went for a walk. Then I called Mrs. Curry, who was surprisingly matter-of-fact. "Found them, have you?" she said. "I'm so glad. Now what?"

I explained the care I was taking not to go public so that she would get at least a third of the value of the papers.

"That's very sweet of you to take all this trouble, Mr. Barley. What can I do to help?"

You would have thought that perhaps three or four hundred thousand dollars would matter more to her, and the thought, or rather, my boss's thought, came into my mind; that she was the mastermind. I brushed it aside, but I was left with a sense that she knew *something* I didn't. I told her about the meeting and she promised to stay home until I called her with the time of it. I called young Gresham to be ready to join us. I forgot that he had no idea of what had happened since I last saw him; when he understood he got very excited. "You *found* them?" he kept saying. "You *found* them?"

I cut him off as soon as I could and walked back to my room. When I opened the door I experienced déjà vu. Something was wrong.

The ceiling was intact, but small chips of plastic foam from one of the panels littered the table; I was sure I hadn't left it like that. I put the chair on the table to go up and have a look, and Tyler walked in.

"That's cute," he said, nodding to the hiding place. "Bring down whatever you've got up there. Let's have a look at it."

"How did you ...?"

"My friend across the street keeps an eye out for me. He just called to say you'd arrived." He gestured at my coat. "Dressed like a rag-picker," he said, "with little glasses. Master of disguise. Now, bring those papers down here."

Brian walked in. "You heard: get those papers down. What have you done with your hair?"

"My girlfriend didn't like it long."

"I thought it was nice."

Tyler said "For Christ's sake. Up you go!"

"Hold on to the chair," I said. I climbed on to the desk and up to the chair and poked my head through the ceiling. "They're not here," I said.

"They're not *what*?!" Tyler was the kind of person who got immediately very angry in such a situation.

I climbed down. "Take a look," I said. "I put them about here." I indicated a place under the ceiling. "There's nothing up there now. Someone's had them. There were plastic crumbs all over the table when I came in."

Tyler said to Brian, "Take a look. I'll hold the chair."

Brian said, "How do I get up on the table?"

I said, "Here." I turned the metal wastebasket upside down to make a step for him and held his hand as he climbed up, holding on to my shoulder with the other hand.

"Hold the chair carefully," he said, and stepped up, poking his head through the ceiling. He climbed down immediately, scrambling to reach the floor as quickly as possible. "They're not there," he said, looking at his hands. "Look at this filth," he squealed. "Don't you have a sink?"

"Where are they?" Tyler demanded.

"I don't know. I put them up there. You saw me starting to look. Somebody else must have seen me. Maybe your sausage guy."

Tyler said, "Where are they, eh, where are they?" His voice got shrill. "Don't give me any more shit."

He came around the table and made a grab at me.

From the doorway Glinka said, "I got your papers."

chapter forty-three

He had what looked like a small cannon in his hand, the barrel about a foot long. "I keep it loaded ever since," he said, waving it over Tyler and Brian.

"Ever since when?" Brian wanted to know.

"Ever since the time they came for me."

"Who? Who came for you? When?"

Glinka looked at him and sucked a tooth, wondering, perhaps, how cloistered Brian's life had been. "The Germans," he said. "In 1944." He weighed the gun in his hand. "I brought it with me when I came to Canada. They didn't have no x-rays on the docks in those days. I've had it ever since. Just in case they come for me again."

Tyler said, "You climbed up there?"

It was a point that was bothering me, too. Eighty years old with only one good hip; it would be tricky.

"They fell down," Glinka said. "The papers. I found the parcel on the table after I heard it crash, so I took a look. It was on the table, all dirty, when I came in to clean. I got it now." He thought of something. "I put the ceiling back with a broom handle."

"Good, fine. You want to get it for us? It belongs to me."

"It belongs to Joe. What do I do, Joe?"

It was time to show our hands. "Call a cab and ask the driver to take it to ... you got a pen?"

"I know the address. Where you work. I'll tell you how later. You hold this while I get the papers." He tried to hand me the gun.

It weighed about ten pounds and felt very unfamiliar. Tyler's face brightened as he began to smell an opportunity, but Glinka was ahead of him. "Here," he said, changing his mind and handing me the keys. "The parcel is in the freezer in the kitchen. Take your time. We'll wait for you."

I ran down the hall and unlocked the door to the stairway, then let myself into Glinka's apartment. The parcel was there, and I grabbed it and a pencil, wrote out the address of my agency on the outside wrapping. I called for a cab and was promised one in twenty minutes, so I told them not to bother and ran out to the street. Harbord is always full of cabs and I got one immediately and sent the parcel on its way. I remembered to wave at the sausage vendor, but he turned his back.

"Now," I said when I was back inside. "We'll meet at two o'clock and talk about the papers, who owns them, stuff like that."

Tyler said, "Could you tell the KGB to go away now?" He pointed to Glinka.

Glinka waved his gun at him. "Don't make jokes like that, okay?" he growled. "I was there." He turned to me. "You okay, now?"

I said, "I think so, Mr. Glinka, thanks." I took out my wallet and found a restaurant receipt and wrote on the back the phone number of the agency. "Call this number at two o'clock, make sure I've arrived. If I haven't, tell Mr. Atkinson what's been happening. He'll know what to do. This man's name is Tyler," I wrote it on the receipt. "Can you read that?"

"I'll manage."

I said to the others, "See you later?" but they were already out the door.

Glinka looked at his gun admiringly. "Sixty years this month. Not bad, eh?" He looked around the room like a man considering having a go at shooting out the light. "You finished now?" he asked.

"Not quite. Tell me what really happened. There's no way those papers could have fallen through the ceiling. I had them wedged in the plumbing."

Glinka shrugged. "I didn't know about you. The guy sells sausages says that you been watching the room. Then you come in with a parcel and go out without it, dressed funny. I called my nephew and he came over and found the parcel in the ceiling, but he says it's nothing, just some stories." He shrugged again. "So my nephew checked a little bit and you're some kind of private detective. So I take a chance. Then I see you come home and I see that turd and his friend come and I listen and hear you need some help. But I can't get the parcel back in the ceiling so I need a little story. Okay? Sorry."

"So I guess I owe you."

"For the week. I have to charge you, I've had inquiries." He turned to go. "Fucking KGB," he said. "What does that dog's turd know about the KGB? He even got the fucking *country* wrong." He limped down the hall, the ancient (East European) gunslinger.

I spent some time collecting Mrs. Curry and briefing her. She took it all very calmly, then said, "Now, I want to buy you lunch. Your office is on the Danforth, you say. You like fish? Good, let's go to Mezzes."

Three times during lunch I tried to talk about the probable value of the papers, and what her share, supposing they agreed to share, would amount to. She brushed the topic aside, wanting to reminisce.

"Are you an antiquarian, Mr. Barley?"

I said I had two first editions of Eric Ambler and a rare paperback of *The Old Dick*, but that was it.

"Well, that's a start" she said. "But let me tell you about a fine edition of *The Moonstone* my husband acquired in an estate sale."

And she did, and about many others. I tried to get back to my current preoccupation, but she didn't seem interested in the Hemingway Papers.

We met in my boss's office: Tyler, Gresham, Mrs. Curry, and Atkinson, my boss. There in the middle of the table sat the Hemingway Papers.

"That's them," Gresham said. "Just like I remember them."

Tyler agreed. "That's the packet I found."

Mrs. Curry said, "Where was that? Where did you find it?"

"Behind the bottom drawer of that old wooden filing cabinet. Not *in* the drawer but wedged behind. The drawer was half-empty and you didn't have to pull it right out to get at everything in it. It was only when I was packing up for the move that I found it, and remembered the history."

"Remembered it belonged to me," Gresham said, looking sharply around the table, like a lawyer on his first case.

"Remembered what it was, and as far as ownership goes, I bought Curry out, lock, stock and barrel, so anything I found was mine," Tyler said.

"Except these papers," Gresham said. "They're mine."

"They're part of the stock I bought."

Mrs. Curry said, "I don't think so. There was an inventory taken prior to the sale—my husband didn't want any misunderstanding. I have a copy of the inventory. These papers aren't on it. They would have been because of their value, but you remember they had already been stolen."

"By your husband, Mr. Curry, from himself, like Tyler did?" Gresham asked. "That's what someone said, though my dad didn't think so."

"That's what a lot of people thought. It doesn't matter. Since he never sold them to Mr. Tyler, I have some claim to them still. What about you?"

Gresham said, "I have a receipt for a thousand dollars in compensation for a loss. My lawyer says the wording is such that it doesn't wipe out my claim. Just shows your husband was trying to be fair. Could we have a look now?"

For him it was like Christmas. I think he was half hoping the manuscript of "The Three Day Blow" would be on top.

Atkinson said to Tyler, "What about you?"

"What's the rule? Possession is nine points of the law? I didn't buy an inventory, I bought the stock. Anything missing from her inventory is a clerical error. It's still part of the sale."

"Not according to my lawyer," Mrs. Curry said.

"Or mine," Gresham said.

"How much are the papers worth?" Atkinson asked.

"I've had an estimate of not less than a million, " Tyler said. "That's with no established provenance."

"What's that mean? With no questions asked?" Atkinson asked.

"More or less. If they came on the open market, they'd fetch more."

Atkinson said, "Even at a million, there'd be enough for the lawyers, and maybe a bit left over."

His point registered quickly. Gresham said, "If it comes out like this, Mum and my lawyer said I was to take a third."

"I would be comfortable with that," Mrs. Curry said.

chapter forty-four

Tyler looked at the papers for a long time before nodding. "Nothing else for it, is there?" He reached out to take the papers, but Atkinson pulled them away.

"You people need to agree and sign the instructions for disposal, and I'll witness it. Then I'll let you have them."

"You're taking a lot on yourself," Tyler said.

"I'm acting on instructions," Atkinson told him.

"Whose?"

"Mine," Mrs. Curry said, smiling like Mona Lisa's mother. "Now, have any of you seen the actual papers? Do you know what Hemingway's handwriting looked like? Open them up, Mr. Atkinson."

Carefully he undid the string and unfolded the brown paper. He lifted the stack of paper clear of its wrapping.

"Top page is blank, a bit brown round the edges," he said like one of those naval officers in the last war disassembling a mine, relaying the instructions step by step to make sure they had learned all they could before the next step blew them up. "The next sheet is also brown at the edges. It's a sheet of typing paper with what looks like the beginning of a story. Listen:

The day was clear and cold and we carried the canoe through the scrub for a mile along the old Indian trail. When we came to the lake we lowered the canoe into the water without setting up any eddies and began casting as soon as we were away from the shore. A big large-mouth hit my bait at the first cast and fought me for twenty minutes before I got a net under him. It stayed like that all day and we caught twenty-seven large-mouth bass and released them all except what we cooked for shore lunch and it was the best fishing I ever had.

"Shall I go on?"

"Just to the next page," Mrs. Curry said.

"The next page is a different colour," Atkinson announced. "Kind of blue. The paper is more brittle, too."

"Show me," Tyler said. He took the sheet of paper over to the window, returning immediately and throwing the paper on the table. "It's a photo copy," he said.

"Not worth a million?" Mrs. Curry asked.

Tyler waited a long time before replying. "It's a curiosity," he said. "It might be worth a few hundred. I don't know."

"That won't keep the lawyers happy, will it?" She burst into giggles. You would not have thought she had a pecuniary interest in the matter.

When I looked up, Gresham was grinning, too. "I think Mr. Curry was having a little fun," he said.

Only Tyler looked black.

"Let us in on the joke, ma'am," Gresham said.

"I won't pretend I didn't know," she said. "I wasn't sure, though, until Mr. Tyler said where he had found it and we got a look at it."

"Sure of what?"

"What you have there is a parcel my husband put together to take to New York when he was looking for offers for the original. Which by the way, he did have once, entrusted to him by Mr. Gresham's father. James, my husband, was nervous about travelling with such a valuable object so he had it copied, put the original in a safe place, and made up a package of the photo copy plus the first page of the original to verify its authenticity. Then someone stole the original." She turned to Gresham. "Someone really did, Mr. Gresham, and when the smoke cleared, my husband, for a joke, I think, as you say, put the copy where you found it, Mr. Tyler, in the hiding place of the original papers. They are still missing, of course. And if they ever turn up, they will belong to Mr. Gresham."

She opened her purse and took out the receipt she had shown me in her apartment. "Here's the receipt my husband got from Mr. Gresham's father. Now look at the date. I'm sorry Mr. Barley, I couldn't resist not pointing it out. I did let you see the receipt, but I was fairly sure you wouldn't realize the significance of the date. Why would you? The receipt is dated two days before the first robbery, which means that Mr. Gresham's claim that the money wasn't given as payment to compensate him for the loss of the papers, but to secure some kind of claim of agency, I think, must be true. My husband just wanted to protect his right to the commission, to sell the papers."

Now Gresham started to laugh, *hoo-hah*s of real merriment. "You're screwed," he said to Tyler. "Sorry, Ma'am."

"Why?" Tyler, who wasn't laughing, asked her. "What's the point?"

Mrs. Curry said, "You have to see things from my perspective. One day you hear or read an announcement that Curry's bookstore has been robbed and valuable books have disappeared. My mind flew back to 1985 as I wondered if finally we were going to recover the papers. I didn't ask, of course, because I knew I would hear, eventually. When Mr. Barley came to see me, I wondered, you know. However, I heard nothing until Mr. Barley brought me up to date and described the package that had fallen into his hands."

I said, "You knew it wasn't the real thing, didn't you?"

"Right away."

"Then why didn't you say so?"

"It would have spoiled the third act, which had to be coming. And so it did." She looked around the table and chuckled, actually made the 'ckl' noise you always read about but almost never hear.

Gresham gave out with another *hoo-hah*.

She stood up. "Well done, Mr. Barley, and thank you. My own feeling is that that single page might be quite valuable, and like the original artefact, it belongs to Mr. Gresham. If you like, Mr Gresham, I'll act as your agent. I still know where to sell it. But I'll agree to whatever you all decide."

"All right?" Atkinson asked, addressing the rest of us.

Gresham stood up. "Sure. Unless the real papers turn up at the back of someone's drawer."

Tyler took more time than the rest of us to get used to the idea that the Hemingway Papers on the table were not what they seemed, and that he had no claim on them anyway. Then he thought of something else. "What do you think my wife hired you for?" he asked me.

I said. "I think I've worked that out. I was supposed to establish your alibi, wasn't I? Testify you were shacked up with your sister-in-law the night the store was robbed."

"But in fact? Go on?"

I couldn't resist it. "In fact, I followed you to the store, watched you stage the break-in, and leave with some books and the papers."

"So I don't have a fake alibi. So I don't have to pay you then."

I said, "I had an associate with me watching the window all the time. Another operative."

Atkinson said, "Another *what*! For God's sake, Joe ..."

"A colleague, a guy from the college. He was my back-up."

"So do we get paid or not?" Atkinson asked.

"Not by me." Tyler leaned back in his chair, pleased at having found a consolation prize.

I said, "There are pictures showing that the other woman is your wife's sister. That something your wife would be interested to know?"

"Not really. We keep it in the family."

"Your wife arranged for her sister to play the other woman?"

"You could say so."

"You just did, in front of witnesses. That's collusion, isn't it?"

"I was joking."

It was like nailing jelly. I said, "I've got timed and dated pictures showing that one night the other woman was, in fact, your wife, standing in for her. Be hard to see that as anything but collusion."

Tyler considered this. "I'll chance it. You won't go to court. And I'll tell you something else. If you're thinking my wife would be shocked by the packet of Jolly Rogers you found in the room, you should know there will be no surprise coming. Take a look out the window." He moved to the window himself and made urgent signalling motions to someone below.

By the time Atkinson and I had reached the window and focused on the sidewalk below, what I now thought of as the Tyler sisters were there, side by side, leaning against the yellow Volvo, waving back.

Tyler said, "The three of us have been sleeping in the same bed, metaphorically speaking, for some time."

I couldn't keep my cool. "*Both* of them?"

Tyler smiled. "So where are the books?" he asked.

The books. I hadn't thought about them since the night of the robbery, so fixated had I become on the papers. The

books were still in my van; I hadn't figured out how to dispose of them yet. I had a notion of sending them to the
insurance company, who, if they had paid Tyler, would
surely own them.

I said, "They belong to the insurance company, don't
they? They pay you and they get to own the books."

He said, "There is no insurance company. I don't have
an insurance policy."

I said, "I don't believe it."

"Could be," Gresham said. "I remember Dad said Mr.
Curry never had one, either."

Mrs. Curry nodded. "Not having insurance is more
common among dealers than you would think," she said.

"So what are we going to do?" I asked Atkinson.

Atkinson said, "You really got the books, Joe?"

I said, "I know where they might be. I'll send them to
the cops."

Atkinson said, "Then it gets messy. They might want
to know where you've been since the night they disappeared. He turned to Tyler. "Pay our bill before you leave.
I'll get it made up. I warn you, we don't come cheap. Then
I'll have a word with Joe about the books. Did you ever
hear the story about the guy in a messy divorce action?
They fought over everything. Finally it came down to who
should get the Mercedes, but they couldn't agree so he proposed that she should sell it and send him half. She did,
sold it for a hundred dollars, and sent him fifty. We'll sell
the books to pay your bill. Should just about cover it. I'll
send you anything left over. I think I know a dealer who
would take them off our hands."

Tyler said, "Those books are worth fifteen thousand
dollars. Make out your fucking bill."

When he left, my boss said, "You never know what's going
on these days, do you, Joe? Even book dealers, eh?"

"You mean crooked dealers? They've been around for a while, surely."

"I know about the crooks. I meant this other stuff." Suddenly, to my amazement, he burst into full baritone song. "How happy could I be with either," he sang. "Were t'other dear charmer away." He stopped, blushing, but pleased with himself. "He's happy with *both*, Joe. And they don't mind. This is your world, not mine. I was born too late for this. You think ..." he paused, looking for the words and the courage to turn the thinkable into the sayable. "You think, maybe, at the same time? He was speaking metaphorically, though, wasn't he? What I was going to say, Joe, is I've never seen any sign of this in Leaside, where I live. Maybe it's all downtown, near you."

"It's unheard of in the Annex. Why, the neighbours in my building are complaining that Carole and I aren't married."

"But that's quite common even in my neighbourhood ... oh, yeah, you're kidding. Right?"

"I guess so. I was thinking about Tyler."

"That's who we're talking about, aren't we."

"He was bragging," I said. "I just realized he's been bragging all along. It's his comic flaw—you know like tragic flaw."

"You mean he isn't diddling both of them?"

"He may be, probably is, but he gets his real kicks out of people knowing it. He's a braggart and an exhibitionist. You know—the clothes, the yellow Volvo. It's the same with that rented room set-up, and hiring me to watch. Like you said once, he could have done it much more simply—if he needed to do it at all—but he couldn't resist showing how smart he was. And he wanted me to see him behind the blind, doing it. Nothing too kinky—just showing off. That was part of it. As for the manuscript, it was the one thing I couldn't understand. In the end, if everything had gone right, he would have had a manuscript to sell, privately. He had that when he first found it, so why complicate things? To show how clever he is, that's why."

"But he isn't, is he? He's just another asshole. Right?"

I had to be fair. "He *was* clever, though. Think about it, a one-night stand complete with pictures on the very night his store is robbed? Even your old colleagues might have been suspicious. But being robbed on one of the many nights he is conducting a serious affair—that's just unlucky. Right?"

chapter forty-five

On Monday morning there was a meeting of the sessionals in the department to hear the candidates declare themselves. The administration still hadn't spoken on the idea of giving us votes. All we had was the original hearsay, that the Board didn't dislike the idea. Our chairman, Fred, trying to gauge precisely the mood of the Board, said, "I would say that they haven't definitely said no to the idea."

Richard was going for broke, canvassing the sessionals, reminding them that it was all his idea.

We assembled at eight in the laboratory theatre. It was a private meeting from which the tenured faculty were excluded, but when the word "secret" began to be heard, Field, our spokesman, and the chairman of the meeting, immediately requested that the tenured faculty appoint an observer. This, he explained to us, would prevent the candidates from speaking with forked tongues, promising one thing to the sessionals and another to the tenured faculty.

His real purpose, though, was to defang that word "secret" which he foresaw would unnecessarily put the administration's backs up.

Field had kept a small section of the front row clear for the candidates, all of whom were present including Riddell, who was reading *Paradise Lost* and chuckling to himself as he made notes in the margin.

As for Field, it was now obvious that we sessionals had utterly failed to see him whole. His size (small, but with wide shoulders as if he had left a coat hanger in his jacket); the little pointed nose; the steel-rimmed glasses, which, though not actually broken, had the look about them of soon to be needing a bit of surgical tape to hold on one earpiece; above all, the sheer geniality of the man, totally undeformed by his experience as a part-timer; all of it contributed to the impression (to us casual observers) that he was aptly named. Field, as in field mouse, a creature I've never seen but which I associate for its sharpness and agreeability with the chipmunk.

It turned out later that Field had taken tea with the president and the chairman of the Board late one afternoon during the week before the election.

The chairman was newly appointed: he was a business graduate of Hambleton who had skipped his way to a dot-com fortune and just as nimbly jumped off the bandwagon with most of his money intact, and had now bought his first radio station.

Hearing a tiny news item on his new wavelength about a fuss among the temporary staff of what he described as "my own campus," he had asked the president to arrange a little informal chat with one of the part-timers, and Fred, picking on Field as the most harmless-looking of us, reported back that Field had represented us very well. At one point he had said to the chairman, "Actually you're running this place on the soundest business principles: the more temporary workers you have, the more flexible you are when it comes to managing the labour force. You should consider paying all the faculty hourly, including these tenured chaps." And they had all laughed.

Now Field swiftly got us seated, told us what we were there for, and asked Daniels to speak.

Daniels spoke for five minutes about what a good chap he was, how hard he worked on departmental committees, and how, if elected, he would bind up our wounds and try to bring the department together to forge a new community for everyone's benefit.

A hand went up, a question. "Could you be more specific? What are you going to do for us, here?"

Daniels said he could not be expected to make specific promises in favour of a small group. The questioner asked why had he come, then, because that was what the group wanted, specific promises.

Jenkins also did himself no good, answering the same question by promising more office space and unlimited use of our offices in the summer, like the tenured faculty.

"Perhaps another washroom, just for the sessionals?" someone shouted, and someone else added, "One of those with a hole in the middle of the floor. You'd only need one."

You could see Jenkins didn't understand and was about to actually consider the suggestion before Field kindly cut him off, laughing loudly to show it was a joke.

Richard was next. It was clear immediately that he was betting on the partial vote coming through and his getting credit for it.

He explained the value of it. "It's the thin end of the wedge," he said. "If two or three of you carry the wishes of your colleagues by combining the partial votes, complete enfranchisement will inevitably follow in the fullness of time."

This was not the angry man I once shared a room with. This was Richard Costril, politician, a cliché in every sentence.

"Will you continue to urge complete faculty suffrage when you are chairman?" someone asked him.

"I shall indeed, acting responsibly, of course, and subject to the constraints of time and energy. We must, of course, avoid spending all our energy between elections revamping the electoral procedures."

Afterwards I realized that at this point he had his eye on the tenured observer. Don't worry, he was saying. There'll be lots of time to talk about it afterwards. I'm not going to change the world overnight.

The effect was that he sounded tricky. He knew it, too, because when he sat down he was searching our faces for reassurance.

Riddell spoke last. He tried not to speak at all, and never actually got to his feet, thus seeming to dispose of whatever chance he had had of getting a single vote. When Field asked him to speak, he smiled and shook his head. "I just came to listen and because you insisted," he said. "I have nothing to say."

Field was equal to him at first. He walked around the front of the laboratory bench and looked at Riddell who was sitting on the platform. "Lay down your Milton," he said, grinning, "and pick up your Burke. Tell us how you would govern us." Field's style included mockery, without being wounding or jeering. He was trying to josh Riddell out of his stance, and it began to work.

Riddell said, "I would govern you, yes. That's the long and short of it. As you know, I don't believe in democracy much, certainly not in an educational institution. To begin with, I don't think the department chairman should be elected at all, but appointed by the dean, to serve at his pleasure."

There was silence, then buzzing, as we took this in.

Then Field said, "We mustn't get too sophisticated. We only have until nine o'clock. So a couple of simple questions. 'What would you do for us, if you were elected.' And, 'Do you think we should have the vote?'"

"I would look after you, of course. That's the responsibility of the ruler. Second, no, as I don't think the rulers should be elected, so I don't see the need for votes."

"Why are you running?"

"It is an accident, a mistake in the minutes of the department meeting. I thought I would let it stand so I could watch what was going on." He smiled. "I'm writing a novel, too."

Field looked slightly less cool. He said, "At least tell us what you think of the current distinction between tenured and untenured staff that has turned us into second-class citizens."

Riddell said, "Oh, I think everyone should have tenure once they are accepted into the community, after a year's probation perhaps, to find out if someone is bonkers. Either that, or abolish tenure altogether. No, it's too late for that. A difficult question, but as far as this arena is concerned it doesn't matter, does it, because we surely wouldn't be permitted to develop our own policy within the department." He looked at his watch. "And now I must go. Don't the rest of you have classes?" He picked up his Milton and left.

Instinctively we waited until the other candidates and the outside observer were gone. Then Field jumped down from the bench. "Now you've heard them," he said. "Much good may it do you."

Later that day every sessional member of the department received a message, in their office, or at home, by letter, phone, fax, or e-mail, to assemble again at eight o'clock the next morning.

chapter forty-six

The corridors vibrated with rumours, settling at last on one, that Richard's gamble had paid off, and the part-timers were to be given a piece of a vote each.

Richard looked very happy as he bustled through the day, sure of reaping the benefit of the new enfranchisement he had helped to bring about, and thus, incredibly, but just possibly, scraping together enough votes from us and the eccentrics to win. By noon he had started his final canvas, a door-to-door campaign of the sessional offices, and by three o'clock he was earnestly soliciting our ideas for his future administration, a Tony Blair among the unions.

Helen Ng, who tutors students in the elements of essay writing, said, "I think Mr. Costril is suffering from early onset Alzheimer's. He's asked me three times today if I need an office of my own in order to talk to my students privately about their syntax."

Ginger said, "I don't trust the fooker. But you can't vote for either of the others, can you?"

It was a sentiment that I was hearing all over. Unlike Tony Blair, Richard had gone too far and outrun his charm. But nobody had a better suggestion.

"You could spoil your ballot," I said to Ginger.

"It goes against my principles," Ginger, the descendant of coal-miners, said. "A vote is a vote."

At eight o'clock, the next morning, Fred, our chairman, asked the outsiders to leave. Richard said, "But surely, Fred, one ought to hear ..."

Ginger said, quietly but clearly, "Fook off now, Richard. Wait 'til you're king," and everyone laughed.

Richard left, and Fred said, "Here is a statement from the chairman of the Board. I will read it to you and leave.

"The Board recently received a request from some members of faculty that the right to cast a vote for a new chairman should be widened to include all faculty, part-time or full-time, who have been with the department at least one year. The proposal suggested that these part-time faculty members should be entitled to vote in proportion to their teaching load.

"Such a proposal encounters two problems.

"First, it treats the faculty in a way to impair their dignity as people. To regard some people henceforth, for this purpose, as one half or two-thirds or some other fraction of themselves and of their colleagues does not attack the idea of first- and second-class citizens that the proposal says it deplores, but confirms it.

"Second, such a principle—votes weighted according to the number of hours taught—if simplistically applied upwards, as it were, would radically reduce the votes of the tenured staff, some of whom have very few actual teaching hours so they can pursue their research interests.

"We see nothing but problems in trying to get an agreement in principle for such a system and in administering it in practice. This is a community of scholar/teachers who should act and be treated as equals. We have therefore decided now that the matter has been brought to our notice, to treat the election of an English department chairman today as an opportunity to put our convictions into practice. All members of the English department, tenured or not, and whatever their current teaching load, who have taught for at least a year, shall be entitled to vote on equal terms with their colleagues. Other departments may see this as the beginning of a new Board policy."

Fred put the paper in his pocket, nodded at us, put up his palm to show he wasn't answering any questions, and left.

Field said, "Voting begins in the chairman's office in ten minutes."

The count took place at ten, and took only a couple of minutes. Riddell won, and promised, as he put it, "To nail the theses to my office door on Friday."

chapter forty-seven

The call came from Mrs. Curry. She said, "Mr. Tyler has asked me to come to the site of his old store this afternoon. He wants me to see something. I wonder if you would come along."

"I haven't been invited."

"I don't want to go alone."

"Why?"

"I don't trust that man. I'll pay you, if you like."

"You've got me curious now. I can pick you up by one-thirty."

"I'll wait for you outside the apartment block. Mr. Gresham will be there, so I think we must be in for some kind of revelation."

"I'm surprised there's anything left of that building. They've been pulling it down for the last three weeks."

"I understand they are dismantling it carefully. A lot of the panelling from the old mansion is still intact and very valuable, as is the flooring. Perhaps Mr. Tyler has found the papers again, under the floor, though I don't think he'd call us together if he did, do you?"

She was waiting for me at the curb, and we made our way to Tyler's bookshop.

There were hoardings around the demolition. Tyler and Gresham waited outside. I found a space to park and Tyler led the way in. Although the ceiling was gone, replaced by a tarpaulin, the shell of the building was still intact and the staircase up to the second floor was still attached to the inside of the wall, like a scene from the Blitz. Two workmen were cleaning the mortar off some loose bricks and stacking them neatly for removal.

"At the back," Tyler said, leading us to the rear of the store. Mrs. Curry followed, with me and Gresham behind.

Tyler stopped by the now-uncovered fireplace. Beside him was a pile of charred paper, mostly ash, but with some triangular fragments intact, the pile covered in a sheet of plastic. Primed as we were, it took us no time to realize we were finally looking at the real Hemingway Papers.

Tyler carefully lifted the plastic sheet. "I thought we should all see this," he said. "George, the foreman, found it and he called me. He'd heard the story. All we've got now is souvenirs. I'm going to put a couple of the scraps under glass in the new shop. How about you?"

I said, "I'd like a piece." I thought I'd take it back for my colleague, David Wintergreen.

Mrs. Curry said, "Thank you, Mr. Tyler. You can have my share. What do you think happened?"

"Was this fireplace boarded up when you had the shop?" Tyler asked.

"Not at first. My husband had it done later to get extra shelf space. We didn't need it, you see, with central heating. But how did the papers get burned?"

"The workmen," Tyler said. "They lit a little fire this morning and the packet fell down into the grate. It was already on fire, so they let it burn. Then the ashes started to blow about so they stamped them out. That's when George noticed the writing and realized it might be interesting. So he called me. I asked Gresham over and we had a look up the chimney in case there were any more rare documents stored there. Take a peek. Not you, Mrs. Curry. You." He pointed at me.

To look up, I had to stand inside the fireplace with your back to the wall. It wasn't clear at first, and then it was. Ten feet above my head what looked like an old suit of clothes seemed to be hung in the chimney where it twisted to continue upwards, the suit wedged in the angle by its shoulders. Then beyond the neck of the suit appeared a skull. The bones of one hand dangled from a sleeve; the other sleeve appeared empty. The legs of the suit hung empty, too. I looked down and saw then the decent cloth with which someone had covered the loose bones—the feet?—that had fallen off the skeleton. I stepped carefully out of the fireplace.

"Let's go downstairs," I said.

When we were assembled on the ground floor, I told the others what I had seen. "How long has it been there?" I wondered.

Tyler said, "About twenty years." He showed us a leather object still identifiable as a wallet. "This was in the grate. One of the workers picked it up. It's Ted Collier, got stuck trying to hide on the night he broke into the safe."

Mrs. Curry said, "You'd better call the police."

"I already did. They said they'll get here as soon as they can. I called the papers and the TV stations, too." He looked pleased with himself; he was going to be on camera, showing how he had discovered Collier and the manuscript. A thought struck him. "We've gone back to square one, right?"

I said, "You tell the story, Tyler. We'll just nod."

Gresham said, "As long as you get the name of my hotel, the Garrick, in there."

Tyler understood and promised and we left.

Outside it was one of those beautiful fall days with just a hint of the winter that was coming, and Mrs. Curry insisted on saying goodbye, to me and Gresham and the Hemingway Papers, with a drink at Le Clochard.

chapter forty-eight

Riddell came in early on Friday morning, nailed his theses to the door (taped them, actually, but made a little drawing of a nail at the top of the sheet) and disappeared before we could question him.

ENGLISH DEPARTMENT

GUIDING PRINCIPLES

In future, the practice of the English department will be governed by the following broad guidelines. I will review these guidelines at the end of the academic year.

Because it usually takes fifty years for works of real value to sort themselves out from the meretricious and the voguish, no course shall be offered that contains works written during the last fifty years.

Every course must be teachable by at least two people, i.e., there shall be no courses that are entirely private to one faculty member.

The students in every course shall be subject to examination by an outside examiner who may set part or all of the examination, and mark a sample of the papers.

Except for the outside examiner requirement in 3 above, all examinations shall be marked in common.

The final grades are recommendations to the registrar only and do not belong to the instructor or the department.

All examinations shall be answerable in essay form.

Please feel free to let me know of anything you think I have forgotten. In the meantime I shall be working on the remaining eighty-nine theses.

J. Riddell

Ginger said, "Now you lot will see some fun."

"Why 'you'?" I asked. "You leaving us?"

"I heard this morning that I'm being laid off at Christmas."

I shouldn't have been surprised. Enough students dropped out in first term every year so that fewer classes were needed, and fewer part-timers.

"What are you going to do?"

Ginger said, "Probably get a job house painting. My dad taught me the trade in the holidays. I hear there's work. But not around here. Seems like a good time to look around. I thought I'd try Vancouver."

epilogue

On the last teaching day of the term, Ginger and I were drinking beer, seated at a table in an outdoor café on Church Street during the Gay/Lesbian parade. Ginger had mentioned it in the office and said he'd like to watch and cheer—there was nothing like that in Scunthorpe, he said, and suggested we make it a farewell lunch, his own. He was leaving on the last day of classes.

It was November, but we were right in the middle of a gorgeous Indian summer, so an al fresco drink seemed very possible. Clouds were piling up over the lake, but it looked as if the rain would hold off for the parade.

When Carole heard she decided to join us. The parade was colourful, noisy, and outrageous as it was every year. It's really an event for new eyes, like Ginger's, and Ginger seemed unable to look away as the parade paced along, arms linked, shouting rude slogans based on the names of politicians they didn't like. Watching Ginger, I wondered if even in Scunthorpe a parade could be that much of a novelty, and then Ginger jumped up, waved, shouted, "There she is!" and pulled me to my feet to show me.

And there she was, Masaka, walking hand-in-hand with a friend, a black-haired woman of her own height, pretty, but occidental, Italian at a guess. She was waving to us.

"Jesus," I said to Ginger. "It's Masaka. What's she doing ... *Jesus!*"

I shut up as I saw that I was exclaiming to two people for whom this was not news. I said to Ginger, "For Christ's sake. Did you know?"

"The first day. When she came to the office. We had coffee. You didn't come 'til the next day. Remember?"

"Did she tell you then?"

"Not in so many words. No, that's a cliché. She told me in so many words. She said, 'I'm not available'."

"You propositioned her?"

"I was just being polite, like. And she cut me off. So I asked her if she was married, or otherwise spoken for, she said she was, but not like that. So I asked her if she was gay, and she said she was."

"Christ! You're lucky she didn't pour her coffee into your lap."

"Mebbe, but she had a reason. Since she was only staying a few weeks she wanted to remain anonymous, because being gay is still interesting to some people, including students, and four weeks isn't enough time for them to get used to it and listen to what she has to say about literature. So she asked me first to keep it to myself, and second to sort of run interference for her."

I turned to Carole. "Did you know?"

"As soon as I met her. I raised an eyebrow, she lowered an eyelid, and we had a pact."

"She swore you to silence, too?"

"Don't be silly. She knew I knew, and I knew she knew I knew, and she knew, and so on. And it was nobody's business but hers."

"Did *I* figure in these understandings?"

"Not in any conversations."

I had a thought. "Did you tell Arlette?"

"Of course not. It's a private thing, as Ginger said."

We watched the parade for a while until I had caught up with the new information. "Anything else everybody knows except me?" I asked.

"I doubt it." Carole stood up. "I have to go." She kissed me, a thing she hardly ever does in public. She turned to Ginger. "Send me a card, will you?' and then *hugged* him, something she absolutely never does, and ran away.

I sat there, looking at the rearranged pieces of my world and trying to make sense of them. After a while, I said to Ginger, "You were really fond of Masaka, weren't you?"

"Am," he said. "She's not dead."

"I always assumed that Masaka was responsible for the new you. But if you knew she was off limits on day one, she couldn't have been."

"The new me?"

"The Sunday clothes when you came to dinner at our place. The lack of women after the first flurry."

"That's what you thought?"

"You were putting on the dog for a Saturday night with me and Carole?"

He said nothing, just looked bleak and watched my face as my own words, or one of them came bouncing back.

"Dear God," I said. "It was Carole, wasn't it?"

He looked away.

"I always wondered how you were so handy when Curry was thumping me. You came looking for Carole, didn't you?"

He said, "You were supposed to be in class."

"Jesus Christ."

Ginger looked over the still passing parade. The first few drops of rain were falling. "I've been on my knees to Carole since the first night you had me over to dinner. I've never met anyone like her."

"What ...?"

"What is it that I like about her?" His voice was tight, hostile. If I said the wrong thing now he would take his misery out on me. "Shall I tell you about her? Describe her, like? Let me count the ways. Ah, shit." He pushed himself away from the table. "And you, you dumb tit, you didn't have the faintest idea, did you?" He managed a small smile. "It ain't right," he added.

I *had* had the faintest idea, though—all those tremors I had misinterpreted. I said, "What will I hear if I tell Carole I've just found out she's been having an affair with you?"

"Haven't you been listening? What I'm saying is that I *haven't* been having an affair with her. I wanted to, but it was no go. I'm still in love with her, but now I'm going away. It'll wear off, I'm sure. There's no problem."

"I'm glad you're going away, though," I said, after a while.

"That's flattering, anyway. Tell me you feel sorry for me and I'll thump you."

"Does Carole know. That—er—you love her?"

"Well, I *did* tell her. You know what she said? No, the hell with it, why should I tell you? Isn't it enough for you that she'll be there when you get home? Now let's change the fookin' subject, shall we?"

But we couldn't think of anything else to talk about, and the rain was starting to come down now, so we walked up to Bloor Street where I caught the subway to Bathurst, and Ginger turned the collar of his jacket up and walked back to his room on Macpherson in the rain.

acknowledgement

My grateful thanks are due to David Mason, who patiently tried to explain to me the rudiments of the rare book trade. He did his best. The howlers left in the book are all mine.